(1,631)

"Comrades have we been in fight; comrades will we be
now the fight is over."

THE LAST OF THE SEA-KINGS

BY

DAVID KER

THOMAS NELSON AND SONS

LONDON, EDINBURGH
DUBLIN, AND NEW YORK

AUTHOR'S PREFACE.

THE real story of Macbeth, from which I have borrowed here, may be found in the notes to Chapter II. of Sir Walter Scott's "Tales of a Grandfather." I have somewhat toned down my hero's Eastern exploits, which, marvellous enough in any case, become quite incredible in the hands of the Norse poets of his time.

DAVID KER.

TO MY DEAR FRIEND AND FELLOW-AUTHOR

MARGARET GEORGE

THIS BOOK IS AFFECTIONATELY
DEDICATED.

CONTENTS.

LIST OF ILLUSTRATIONS.

THE LAST OF THE SEA-KINGS.

CHAPTER I.

FIGHTING THE STORM.

FIERCELY swept the north-east gale along the eastern coast of Scotland on a wild March morning in the stormy spring of 1039, howling through the leafless trees, and piling the great waves of the North Sea in leaping hills of foam on the grim black rocks of that iron-bound shore.

Well might the few fishermen who, just where the busy port of Leith now stands, had dragged their rude boats ashore under the lee of a sheltering point, shake their heads and look meaningly at each other as they caught a glimpse of the solitary vessel which, half seen through lashing spray and blinding rain, was driving headlong before the gale over the wild waters of the Frith of Forth, all but hidden ever and anon by the mountain billows that raged around her.

A very strange - looking craft she would have appeared to any seaman of our time; but in those days such a ship was an only too common sight on every coast of Western Europe.

She was simply a huge row-boat, with a line of big, heavy oars along either side, not a few of which had already been broken, strong as they were. All along her low bulwarks, over which the sea broke every moment in roaring floods of foam, glittered rows of shields belonging to the warriors who manned her; and she had but a single short, clumsy mast, which, stripped of its one huge sail, and broken off at the top, told how sorely she had been battered by the storm that she was striving to escape.

But there seemed to be little hope of escape for her; for neither oar nor rudder could check her headlong rush right toward the two perilous head-lands which, only a few miles away, guarded the sides of the narrow, winding strait through which the river Forth pours itself into the wider frith beyond.   On one or the other, as it seemed, she *must* strike; and to strike was certain destruction.

As man after man along the shore caught sight of her, cries of excitement flew from mouth to mouth, and many a hard brown hand clutched at knife, hatchet, club, boat-hook, or any other weapon within reach.

And well might it be so, for in that fierce age there were few men who were not familiar with the build and rig of those terrible northern pirate-ships that were the scourge of every coast from Stockholm to Gibraltar. So cruelly had England, and Scotland in particular, suffered from their ravages that in every church of Britain, from Kent to Orkney, daily prayers arose for "deliverance from the rage of the Vi-kings" (sea-kings); nor could any man within twenty miles of the sea lie down to sleep with any confidence that he might not awake to find himself bleeding to death amid the ruins of his blazing home, while his wife and children were dragged away to hopeless slavery.

But the panic subsided as quickly as it had arisen; for one glance told the experienced lookers-on that no harm was to be feared from a vessel that was herself on the very brink of destruction.

"She'll ne'er weather Black Ness," muttered a rough-looking fellow, who was keenly watching her course. "Yet another half-hour, and these venture-some voyagers will all be feeding the fish of the frith."

"Let them!" growled a second man; "it is just what they deserve. These northern ravens have been tearing our land in pieces this many a day, and now it is their turn to be torn in pieces in like manner."

By this time the struggling ship was far past the isle of Inchkeith; and now she rounded Inchcolm in turn, and, losing sight of the high ridge from which, two miles to the south, the huddling hovels and rude timber fort of Edwinsburg (the future Edinburgh) looked down on the wild waste of waters, went flying onward, straight toward the nearest of the two fatal headlands, which was now looming out right ahead of her, plainer and plainer every moment, through driving mist and pelting rain.

Meanwhile, how fared it with the doomed men on board of that helpless vessel, who were thus face to face with seemingly certain death?

To all appearance, in truth, they had absolutely no chance of life left; for even should they, contrary to all expectation, escape the fury of the sea, they had no mercy to hope for from the enraged natives, who had suffered from their pitiless raids so long and so cruelly.

But even with death in its worst form staring them in the face, these reckless rovers showed no sign of gloom or despair. So far from that, in fact, they answered the howling and shrieking of the gale with bursts of ringing laughter, and kept defying with rough jests the ceaseless battering of the great waves against the trembling planks beneath their feet; while a tall, handsome young man who was steering (a task that strained his utmost strength, great as it was, to control the furious leaping and jerking of the rudder) uplifted a voice as deep and powerful as the roar of the storm itself to chant an old northern war-song, which may be translated somewhat as follows :—

> " The rocks of old Norway
>   Are worn by the sea ;
> The high castle towers
>   Dust and ashes shall be.

> " The trees of the forest
>   Must fall by the steel ;
> The swift-flying eagle
>   The arrow must feel.

> " Bright swords shall wax rusty,
>   Fine gold shall grow dim ;
> The ale-cup be tasteless
>   Though filled to the brim.

> " The earth and its glory
>   Must vanish one day ;
> The soul of a hero
>   Endureth for aye ! "

And now they were but a hundred yards from the perilous point, and now but fifty; and now there broke through rain and mist and spray, close under their lee, a sudden ghastly vision of cruel black rocks, and white, gnashing breakers, and leaping foam, and deafening uproar.

A terrific plunge, a mighty shock, a violent turn of the rudder——which tasked to the utmost the strength of the young steersman and of another man who sprang to help him——and then all at once, they knew not how, the grim rocks and furious waves lay many yards behind them.

"King Ægir" (the sea) "is balked this time, anyhow," chuckled a stalwart young Norseman in the bow, as he looked back at the vanishing headland that they had so narrowly escaped.

"Ay, lad; but he who breaks the Laeding chain may yet be bound by the chain of Dromi," * gravely replied an older man beside him, with a meaning glance at the long black fang of the Wolf's Head, which, white with lashing waves, was now looming out right ahead of them in its turn.

In fact, marvellous as their escape had been from the rocks of the southern headland, it seemed as if nothing short of a miracle could save them from the

* "He who breaks the Laeding chain may be bound by the chain of Dromi" is a Norse proverb answering to our "You may go farther and fare worse," the allusion being to the two chains forged by Thor to bind the demon Fenrir.

northern one, which they had still to pass. So far did it extend southward across the strait that it was not possible to weather it without making so wide a sweep as would almost certainly run them aground on the fatal sands of the southern shore.

But the sturdy Norsemen never wavered for an instant. Then, and for many years later, the special horror of every Norse or Danish warrior was what he called " a cow's death "—that is, dying a natural death in his bed—and a violent end by battle or storm, so far from being feared, was looked forward to with the greatest eagerness, as the only death fit for a man. Nor had Christianity (though already the established religion of a great part of the far north) done much as yet to soften the fierceness of these wild converts, though it was to bear glorious fruit in after days.

One chance, however, the bold men had on their side in this match with death. The northern warships were always built lightly and with little draught of water, to enable them to go up friths and river-mouths, or to enter shallow lagoons; and thus, though it was hardly possible for their vessel to clear the strait without touching shoal or rock, she might scrape over it or be lifted off it by a wave, where a larger and heavier ship would be hopelessly stranded.

With a cheery shout the men bent to their oars;
and their young leader at the helm, while glancing
warily to right and left as he steered, uplifted once
more his stirring chant, which was lustily echoed,
through the roar of wind and wave, by not a few
deep voices among the crew.

> " Our bones may lie bleaching
> On bleak battle-plain ;
> Our armour be rusted
> By mist and by rain ;
>
> " Our ships may be broken
> By billow and blast ;
> The fame of our glory
> For ever shall last ! "

Up and down, up and down—now whirled aloft
on the crest of a mountain billow, now plunging
down again, with a dizzy, sickening rush, into a deep
dark valley between two great hills of water—but
ever nearer, nearer, nearer still to the deadly strait
between the rocky headland and the hidden shoals,
while the pelting spray scourged their smarting eyes,
and the furious wind seemed to strangle them at
every breath.

All at once a quivering shock ran through the
whole vessel from stem to stern, and at the same
moment came from beneath the very feet of the
doomed crew that harsh, grating, grinding noise which,

once heard, can never be forgotten—the sound which tells that a ship's keel has touched sand or rock.

For one instant the life of every man on board hung by a thread ; and then one tremendous stroke of the oars, aided by a mighty wave which just then came rushing on, forced the light vessel right over the perilous reef, and swept her through the deadly strait into the calmer waters of the sheltered river beyond.

Little dreamed the exultant rovers, in the first glow of this unhoped-for deliverance, that all Norway, and all England too, would one day curse the hour of their escape, and would wish that their storm-tossed ship had carried with her to the depths of the sea the one fated life that was hereafter to bring death to thousands.

CHAPTER II.

LAND-WOLF AND SEA-WOLF.

SO startling and bewildering was this sudden passage from death to life that for one moment even the reckless sea-rovers stood silent and amazed; and then their simple, boyish exultation found vent in a lusty shout of "Yuch-hey-saa-a-a!" —the ancestor of our "Hip-hip-hurrah!"

But the cheer had hardly died away when the daring men found to their cost that they were exulting too soon.

True, they were now in smoother water, and somewhat sheltered from the fury of the gale by the high ground above them; but, on the other hand, the discoloured water all around them told at once to their practised eyes that they were traversing a perfect network of sandbanks; and, moreover, a hoarse voice was heard to announce, just at that moment, that the ship had sprung a leak!

"No matter!" cried their young captain, as cheerily as ever; "we must just run her ashore, then, in the first likely place that we can find; and then we will go up to that tower that I see on yon hill and ask shelter; and if they refuse it, we will take the tower by storm, and harbour there till we can make the *Serpent of the Sea*—that is, the ship—fit to sail again."

A hearty cheer applauded this bright idea, which seemed quite reasonable to these wild men, even when just snatched from apparently certain death. To them, in whose eyes the whole earth was a mere hunting-ground, where all belonged to him who could seize, it seemed the most natural thing in the world that when they wanted anything they should go and take it from some one else who had it; and if there were a chance of their being killed in doing it, so much the better sport!

Such was the raw material from which, when refined by civilization and softened by Christianity, was one day to be wrought the empire of Britain.

At the cheering prospect of a desperate battle the drenched, weary, half-starved men brightened up amazingly. Wet and cold as they were, a little hard fighting was the very thing to warm them up; and if forty stout Norsemen could not match—

ay, and overmatch too—the garrison of any castle on that coast, it would be a very odd thing indeed.

While some of them baled out the water that kept rushing in through the leak, and others toiled at the oars, the young chief resumed his post at the helm; and on they flew, still running before the wind (though with abating speed) and looking keenly on every side for a place to beach their vessel, though as yet it was nowhere to be found.

Twice they grounded on the encircling sandbanks; twice the staunch little craft tore herself free again, and swept on once more; and ere long they were near enough to the castle to see that it was even stronger than they had thought, which, so far from quenching their eagerness to attack it, only made them more eager than ever.

All at once a cry of excitement was heard from a man in the bow, echoed instantly by three or four of his comrades with one voice.

The young chief who was steering looked up quickly, just in time to see a human form come bursting through the matted thickets that covered the higher part of the sloping shore, and rush frantically down the incline toward the beach, glancing back over his shoulder as he did so, as if pursued.

Pursued indeed he was (as soon became evident) by the deadliest and most untiring of all foes.

The hunted fugitive was barely half-way from the thicket to the water's edge when a harsh, horrible yell rent the air (at the sound of which the approaching Norsemen gave a start of sudden recognition), and out from the crackling boughs of the undergrowth broke open-mouthed, in hot pursuit, three monstrous wolves !

Then, and long after, these fell destroyers were the pest of all Scotland ; for while in England the "gray beast of the forest " was speedily exterminated, in the thinly-peopled north it held its ground so long that not till late in the seventeenth century did the last wolf fall by the hand of Black Evan Cameron of Lochiel.

The beasts were manifestly gaining on their flying prey—the foremost wolf was already at the fugitive's heels, and the other two were close behind—when this man-hunt (which the sea-kings watched with breathless interest from their ship) took a new and startling turn.

Quick as thought the runner faced about, and, with the light hunting-spear that he carried, dealt so fierce a thrust at the nearest wolf that it ran right through the gaunt gray body from side to side, and dug itself into the earth beyond !

With the force of the blow the steel head snapped

short off; but down came the spear-shaft with
crushing force on the extended fore paw of the
second wolf as it sprang at him, and the crippled
beast rolled over with a howl of pain. Then he
hurled the shaft at his third assailant with a shock
that checked its rush for a moment; and ere it
could seize him, he had reached the place of refuge
that he was striving to gain.

This was an upright pillar, or rather slab, of gray,
moss-clad granite, about ten feet high, which stood close
to the water's edge——probably the last relic of one of
those famous " circles " once so common in many parts
of Scotland, and still to be found in the Orkney Isles.

Up it he scrambled like a wild cat. Not a whit
too soon, for just then the pursuing yell broke out
again, louder than ever, as the rest of the pack were
seen coming tearing down the slope at full gallop;
and instantly all below him was one whirl of shaggy
gray bodies, and snapping jaws, and whisking tails,
and foul, greenish-yellow, murderous eyes.

In clambering up the great stone, the hunted
hunter had turned right toward the coming ship;
and her crew, who were now pretty close to the
scene of action, saw with amazement that the hero
of this daring feat was a smooth-faced boy !

In their honest admiration of his courage, the

bold sea-kings set up a shout that made the air ring,
and for a moment startled the wolves from their
prey. But hunger overcame even the beasts' native
cowardice, and they darted on the forlorn lad once
more, some leaping up in the air to snap at his feet,
while others rushed again and again up the rugged
surface of the great boulder, hoping to clutch him
and drag him down.

Thus assailed on every side, and perched on a
slippery stone where there was barely room for him
to stand, the boy's danger seemed even greater than
before; and at sight of his peril, the fiery young
captain of the Norse warship lost patience altogether.

" He shall not perish unaided!" cried he vehemently.
—" Catch hold of the helm, Saemund."

" Bide thee, Feeder of the Ravens ! " said the old
seaman to whom he spoke ; " he who leaps without
looking catcheth a fall. Thou canst not fight a
whole wolf pack single-handed ; bide thee till we
can all go at them together."

" And meanwhile yon brave lad will be torn in
pieces ! " cried the young man fiercely. " Ere I let
such a champion be made wolf's meat before my
very eyes, they shall devour me too, body and bones!"

And he plunged at once into the swirling waters
below.

This of itself was no light hazard, for the meeting of the inrushing tide and the outrushing river had stirred up a battle of contending waters from which even a strong swimmer might well have shrunk. But the young giant, though weighed down not only by his clothing, but also by his steel cap and the axe in his belt, buffeted the waves right manfully, and setting up a cheery shout as he felt his feet touch ground, struggled onward to the shore, and without a moment's pause sprang right into the midst of the leaping, yelling monsters.

Twice the terrible axe flashed and fell, and at each blow fell a wolf. But the rest closed round him open-mouthed, and he had barely time to set his back against the great boulder and sweep his battle-axe right and left, like a scythe, through the leaping wave of glaring eyes and lolling tongues and sharp white fangs that surged up all round him.

"Aoi! Aoi!" he shouted, awakening every echo of the encircling hills with the roar of the Norse war-shout, while cries and howls and crashing bones answered every stroke of the fatal axe.

But the bold lad above, at sight of his rescuer's peril, lost all thought of his own safety. Wrapping his gray mantle round his left arm as a shield, he clutched his broad-bladed dirk with the other, and

with a ringing shout leaped down into the thick of
the fray.

In a moment more the two young heroes stood
shoulder to shoulder, with their backs to the great
stone, slashing right and left with the force of giants
at their swarming, howling foes, as if hacking their
way through a thicket.

But such a combat could not last. Though at
least a dozen wolves lay dead around them, the rest
seemed only to wax more furious. Already the
boy's right shoulder was bleeding from a cruel bite,
and a dark stream was oozing through the torn
bearskin leggings that covered his ally's limbs to
the knee; and nothing but the ceaseless sweep of
their weapons (which was too exhausting to be kept
up long) saved them from being torn to rags on
the spot.

But help was now at hand. The wary old
Saemund, left to manage the helm, was quick to
see that here, at last, was a place where the ship
might be safely beached; and one dexterous turn
of the rudder drove her right up on to the sand, close
to the scene of the combat.

Out poured the Norse rovers, with a thundering
shout, over the low side of the careened vessel, and
splashing through the shallow water, flew axe in

hand to their leader's aid. At the same moment an answering cheer rang out from the crest of the ridge above, and a score of sturdy fellows, armed with long spears, came charging down the slope to the rescue.

Then for a few fierce moments spear and axe worked unsparingly, till the few wolves that had escaped the slaughter fled howling away; and among the carcasses of the dead monsters the two heroes of this death-grapple—weary, wounded, gasping, stained with blood—stood triumphant amid a shouting throng.

"Thou art my brother from this day, young Kiempe" (champion), cried the Norse captain, as he seized the boy's hands in his own. "Comrades have we been in fight; comrades will we be now the fight is over. By what name do men call thee? it is no unworthy one, I trow."

"I," said the lad, returning his cordial grasp with equal heartiness, "am Kenneth Macduff of Dun-na-mairl, son of the Thane of Fife."

"And I," said his new friend, "am Harold, Sigurd's son, Prince of Norway."

CHAPTER III.

A COUNTRY GENTLEMAN OF THE ELEVENTH CENTURY.

WHILE the two champions were thus speaking together, young Macduff's followers and Prince Harold's sea-rovers were eyeing each other doubtfully, very much as two strange dogs might do when uncertain whether to make friends or to fight.

In truth, it would have been nothing surprising in that stormy age if the two parties, heated as they were by their fight with the wolves, had flown at each other's throats there and then, and fought till the last man went down. But when the men on either side saw their leaders exchange so friendly a greeting, they too began to mingle together like comrades, and to salute each other with rough, good-humoured jests.

When, however, they heard the Norse chief name himself as " Harold, Sigurd's son, Prince of Norway,"

a murmur of surprise and admiration buzzed
through the band of Scottish spearmen, and
Kenneth Macduff himself glanced at his rescuer
with a new interest.

In fact, the young sea-king was well worth
looking at.

Youth as he was (for he could hardly be more
than nineteen) he towered a full head above the
tallest of the stalwart forms around him, fully
bearing out the reports that made him more
than seven feet high; and the great knots of
muscles that stood on his bare arms and limbs
amply accounted for the amazing force that he
had shown in the combat.

Giant as he was, however, there was nothing
heavy or ungainly in the grand proportions of
his massive frame; and though his hands and
feet were unusually large (a very rare thing in a
Norse warrior), they were undeniably well shaped.
His all but beardless face (the fresh ruddiness of
which had been but slightly browned by sun
and storm) was beautiful as the fabled Baldur
of northern legend; and the large blue eyes, that
looked out from beneath the long golden hair
which hung tossing like a mane over his head
and shoulders, were bright with a frank, fearless,

boyish good-humour that was indescribably attractive, though a slight inequality in one eyebrow (which was a trifle higher than the other) gave a somewhat stern look to his noble features when in repose.

"What?" cried Kenneth at last, recovering from his surprise, "art thou the hero of Stikelstad, whose fame all the harps of the north resound? for that he, a fourteen-year-old boy, fought by his brother's side till he was stricken down and left for dead."

"Of such fame am I not yet worthy, though I hope to do better anon," said the young prince modestly—for, even in his hot youth, the great conqueror was singularly free from that childish boastfulness which was in that age the chief failing of his countrymen; "but I am indeed he of whom thou speakest."

"Ye be Christian folk, then?" said young Macduff, with a meaning side look at Harold's band of sea-rovers, whose wild forms and grim faces, and disordered clothing, dripping with brine, and smeared with dust and blood, certainly looked as little Christian-like as could well be.

"Christian folk we be, even as ye," said Harold; "and therefore do I crave of thy kindness, brother

Kenneth, as warrior from warrior, and as Christian
man from Christian man, some fire to dry my
men's wet clothes, and some food for their need."

"Food and fire shalt thou have, and welcome,
and aught else of which thou hast need!" cried
the young Scot heartily; "it is not every day,
I trow, that our roof harbours such a guest.
Come with me."

And forthwith Scots and Norsemen—who a
minute before had been ready to knock each
other on the head, and who might actually do
so at any moment, if occasion arose—were tramping
off together, joking and laughing as if they were
the best friends in the world; while young Macduff,
having left a dozen or so of his men to look after
the stranded ship, and see that no one tried to
plunder it, went up the hill side by side with
Harold himself.

As they mounted the slope the young sea-king,
in his turn, took a fuller survey of his newly-
adopted "brother" than he had yet had time
to make.

Kenneth Macduff was a ruddy, auburn-haired
lad of fourteen, very tall for his age, though he
looked a mere child beside the giant sea-king.
His spare frame and gaunt limbs contrasted very

strikingly with the Norseman's mighty bulk; but Harold's practised eye saw in that slender form a sinewy strength and elasticity that might be a match for many a far larger man. The young Scot's face, if not handsome, had a bright, open, hearty freshness that pleased Harold well; and as the lad's keen gray eyes looked trustfully into his own, the young prince, already no mean judge of men, inwardly decided that this new comrade of his would be a friend worth having.

Just as they reached the brow of the ridge the two friends saw hurrying toward them a shouting throng of men, bare-footed and bare-armed, some brandishing spears, some waving short swords, and not a few wielding rude clubs newly cut from the trees, with the bark still on them.

Their dress was as motley as their weapons. Some were clad in rough wolfskin or bearskin coats; others wore cowhides, with the hair turned inward; and several had no clothing but a close-fitting white-gray tunic with two holes for the arms, which looked very much like a torn meal sack.

At sight of them Macduff smiled in quiet amusement, and Harold broke into a hearty, boyish laugh; for he guessed at once that this rude

militia had seen his ship in the distance, and were
hastening, with such arms as they had, to repel,
as they thought, a pirate raid.

In fact, the advancing Scots, as soon as they
caught sight of the Norse helmets and battle-
axes coming over the crest of the ridge, set up
a louder shout than before, and closed up as if
for the onset. But when they saw young Macduff
and Prince Harold walking side by side in such
friendly wise, and so many of their own men
mingled familiarly with the rovers, they stopped
short with an air of blank bewilderment.

" No need of weapons this time, clansmen," said
Kenneth, smiling. " These are comrades and guests,
and this chief is my friend and my brother."

" And if the friendship be as long as the
friend himself, it must needs last a good while,"
said a big, red-haired peasant, eyeing with an
admiring grin Prince Harold's seven feet odd of
bone and muscle.

No one laughed more heartily than Harold
himself at this blunt jest, which was quite in
the spirit of an age when all men spoke their
minds freely, and he replied, good - humouredly
enough,—

" Ye Scots have little to fear from any foe,

methinks, if ye be ever as prompt as now to
defend your coasts; but I trow I and my men
have been too busy this day in saving our own
lives to have much thought of taking yours.
Yonder lies our ship, but it would profit ye
little to plunder her; there is naught left on
board worth taking."

"Nay, the plundering we leave to thee," chuckled
the red-haired wag; "ill can the moorcock match
the raven at thieving!"

"As little," retorted Prince Harold, "as the
raven can match the moorcock at crowing!"

The laugh was now turned against the joker
himself, who joined in it with a right good will;
for in those days it was a point of honour to
bear a hard hit well, whether of word or of blow.

"Be there any good wars toward in these parts,
comrade?" asked the young prince as they
moved on again, in just the same tone in which
a lad of our time might ask if there were any
cricket matches in the neighbourhood.

"None worth telling of," said young Macduff
regretfully; "but I trow we shall have some
sport ere long, for these Northumbrian neighbours
of ours are a restless folk, and seldom give our
weapons time to rust."

In our own day — even with the "northern
express" accomplishing in a few hours the journey
that once took weeks and months—it might well
startle any one to hear a lad north of Edinburgh
talk of the Northumberland people as his neighbours.
But it was then the literal truth; for the great
Saxon earldom of Northumbria extended (as its
name implies) north from the Humber right up
to the Forth (including Edinburgh itself), while
to the west of it Strathclyde came down from
the Clyde's mouth almost to the border of what
is now Lancashire; and "Scotland," as it then
was, meant only the irregular triangle of mountain
and forest lying between the Clyde and the Forth
on one side and the great northern sea on the
other.

By this time they were close to the castle,
at which the young sea-king looked with all
the interest natural to one who had so lately
been thinking of attacking it himself, and he
was fain to own that it would have been "a
very hard nut to crack."

The outer wall occupied the entire summit of
an isolated bluff overhanging the river, so steep
that only two of its four sides were accessible
at all; and even there the narrow, zigzag, break-

neck path, by which only two men could mount abreast, was exposed to a storm of arrows not only from the first wall, but also from a higher one within it.

Between the outer and the inner wall lay the great courtyard, beyond which, within the second rampart, stood the house itself.

This, unlike the tall towers introduced into Britain by the Normans some thirty years later, was a long, low building of dark-gray stone, but one story high, around which clung a growth of timber "lean-to" sheds, serving as barns, cow-houses, storerooms, and what not. At one end of this building rose a round, massive loop-holed tower, evidently meant for the citadel of this primitive fortress, into which the garrison, when all else was taken, might retreat to prolong their defence.

"My father is gone a-hunting," said Kenneth Macduff, as they came up to the foot of the ascent; "but he will be back, methinks, ere the even meat be set on the board, and meanwhile I wot well that my mother will give thee and thy men a right Scottish welcome."

"I doubt it not," said Prince Harold courteously. "And blithe will we be to have it, for we have

not tasted bite or sup this day; and I, for one,
am as hungry as Logi in the old saga [story],
who, when set down to a trough of meat, ate
not only the meat, but the bones and the trough
as well!"

As he spoke, Kenneth blew the horn that
hung at his side. Instantly an answering blast
came echoing from the castle above, a head
showed itself over the outer wall, a few words
were exchanged, and then the heavy gate swung
slowly open, and into the courtyard tramped
the two leaders and their train, with their weapons
flashing and sparkling in the slanting sunlight;
for by this time the afternoon was beginning to
wane into evening.

It soon appeared that young Macduff had said
no more than the truth in promising his new
friends a hearty welcome from his mother. Forth
from her "bower" (a large room to the left of
the hall, in which she and Kenneth's two young
sisters were sitting together) came Dame Granua
(Grace), who, if less refined than the Lady
Macduff into whom Shakespeare has idealized
her, had all the frank hospitality of the Middle
Ages, and a very warm heart of her own to
boot; and she received with overflowing kindness

the gallant young Norse chief whose name was already renowned over all Scotland.

In a trice the drenched and hungry Norsemen were gathered round a blazing fire in the great hall, which soon dried their dripping clothes; and while the friendly warmth put new life into their numbed limbs, their eager eyes lighted up at sight of the rude abundance of good cheer piled on the long tables around them for the evening meal, which was served half an hour earlier than usual in honour of their coming.

" Well, this is a snugger harbour than the bottom of the sea, anyhow, eh—Biorn ? " said Sweyn, Eric's son (a big, hard-faced old gray-beard who held the post of doctor to this respectable ship's company), as he rubbed his brawny hands gleefully over the cheering fire.

" Right, comrade," chuckled Biorn (Bear), a tall, gaunt, sinewy, long-limbed fellow, nicknamed " Hare-foot," from his swiftness in running. " Of the two, I had rather eat fish and fowl "—and he cast a hungry look at the dainties around him— " than that fish and fowl should eat me ! "

" That wolves should eat thee, thou meanest," chimed in a shorter man by his side, with a scarred face and keen bright eye, known as

"Nine-man Mord" (nine men's death), from his having overcome in one battle nine foes in succession. "But, in truth, we have had fair welcome in this Scottish land, where we looked but for point of spear and edge of sword, and meet it is that we should thank this young jarl [earl] as befits warriors.—How say'st thou, Jarl?" added he, turning to young Macduff. "Wilt thou take ship with us when we sail again, and come away over the swan's bath [the sea] to seek red gold and fair adventures? Right gladly will we have thee for our comrade!"

This idea of showing their gratitude by inviting their host, a lad of good family, to leave his home and turn pirate, was in that age, absurd as it may appear to us, quite a reasonable suggestion. Then, and long after, piracy was the recognized career for any promising young man in Norway or Denmark; and any careful father who had a son to provide for was wont to "give him a long ship" and send him buccaneering, not seldom with the plain-spoken farewell of grim old Jarl Rognwald to his son Einar: "It were well if thou never comest back."

"Thanks, good friends," said Kenneth, taking Mord frankly by the hand. "In good sooth, there is naught that I should like better than to sail the seas in the company of such champions as ye be; but it is for my father to decide that matter, not for me. Without his leave and his blessing go I no whither."

"Well said, brother Kenneth!" cried the prince, who was standing by him; "but have no care on that score. As soon as thy father returns, I myself will ask leave for thee to go a-sailing with us, and I trow he loveth thee too well to refuse."

The young chief had not long to wait for the testing of that fatherly love which must be too strong to balk his only son of so fine a chance to turn pirate. As young Macduff had foretold, supper was not yet ready ere the blast of a horn was heard outside, echoing and re-echoing among the encircling hills as if it would never end.

"It is my father's horn," cried Kenneth, darting out, "and the blast tells that he has had luck in his hunting."

He flew through the inner gateway, and had just reached the great courtyard, when its huge gate swung heavily back, creaking and groaning, and the last lingering gleam of sunset on the hilltops showed him a train of wild figures pouring in, laden with the heads and quarters of deer.

Conspicuous among them was a tall, fine-looking man of middle age, who made a stately and imposing figure even in his rough hunting-dress, smeared as it was with dust and blood, and badly torn to boot. Toward him young Macduff flew with extended hands, for this man was no other than his own father, the great "Maormor" or Thane of Fife.

"Welcome, son Kenneth!" said the elder Macduff, greeting his boy with a hug worthy of a polar bear. "I bring thee good news, lad—news of war!"

CHAPTER IV.

THE COMING OF THE RAVENS.

MACDUFF'S announcement of what he was pleased to call "the good news of war" reached no ear but that of his son. And the father's warning gesture came just in time to check the gleeful shout that the boy was about to utter; for in that fierce age, alas! tidings of havoc and ruin were always looked on as an occasion of joy, not of mourning.

"Hold thy peace yet awhile, son," said he; "thou shalt know more anon. Hark ye, what is this that I hear of guests whom thou hast brought home? Certain of our clansmen met me on the way, who spake of having seen thee leading hither a band of Norsemen from a wrecked ship."

Kenneth, in his turn, told, in a few simple, stirring words, the tale of the day's adventures, to which his father listened with close attention.

"What—Harold Sigurd's son of Norway?" cried

he at last. "Better comrade at need there can be
none; nor could he have come in a better hour.
And he hath saved thy life, then ? Go quickly and
bid him welcome from me, and see that he be well
cared for; and say to him that, as soon as I have
spoken a word with thy mother, I will myself come
and thank him for helping thee."

This was speedily done, in the frankest and heart-
iest manner, and a few minutes later the Thane
of Fife, having "dressed for dinner" with phenomenal
quickness, considering what a pickle he had been in
when he came home, was seated at the head of his
own board, between his lady and Prince Harold.
Next to Harold sat Kenneth Macduff; and the Scots
and Norsemen, all mixed up together, were ranged
along the tables lower down—the total company
numbering nearly a hundred.

Could an exact picture of that banquet-hall have
been preserved for us, it would have greatly amazed
any one used to the dinner-parties of our day; for
the dirtiest London tavern would seem a palace to
the dining-room of this powerful noble.

The low, massive cross-beams of the roof were
literally caked with soot from the huge fire of peat
that burned in the middle of the floor, rolling its
smoke in stifling volumes through the entire hall, to

escape at last by a hole in the roof. From the fire itself, as well as from the pine-wood torches that blazed and crackled overhead, showers of sparks fell unceasingly on the rough dress and shaggy hair of these wild feasters; and amid the dirty, half-rotten rushes, that covered the floor in place of a carpet, lay countless bones that had been picked clean by the big, hairy wolfhounds which were couched around the fire.

This bone museum was constantly receiving new additions of a very curious kind. In that simple age, when forks were unknown, and for knives gentlemen used the daggers with which they had probably stabbed a man not long before, the usual way to peel a bone properly was to gnaw the meat from it with one's teeth, and then fling it at the head of one's opposite neighbour—this bone-pelting being a regular feature of every northern dinner-party in the tenth and eleventh centuries. As may be supposed, the dogs snapped greedily at the flying bones as they fell, and their barking and growling over these dainties mingled with the hoarse shouts and laughter of the noisy guests; and, to crown all, the old family bard, who stood behind Thane Mac-duff's seat, kept thrumming on a huge harp strung with bears' sinews set in brass, and singing an

interminable ballad, which, like most songs of that
age, was all about fighting and throat-cutting.

For some time not a word passed between Macduff
and the Norse leader; for in that age nothing was
thought so rude as to ask a guest's business, or even
his name, unless he chose to tell it himself, ere he
had had his fill of meat and drink. But at last the
thane rose from his seat, and, filling a huge horn
to the brim, called out loud enough for every one
to hear,—

"Skoal [health] to the sea-king and to his men.
Our ears are open for the tale of what great deeds
they have done, and what has brought them to our
coast."

Harold bowed his lofty head courteously, drained
the horn in turn, and then reaching out his hand for
the harp, which the bard, who had by this time
ended his song, at once handed over to him, he began
to chant, in a voice of amazing power and volume,
though rich and musical withal, one of the improvised
songs for which in after years he was as famous as
for his countless feats of strength and valour.

First he sang of the fatal battle of Stikelstad (the
last grapple of heathenism and Christianity in Norway), where his brother King Olaf had fallen.

He told how the hero-king, hemmed in by a

mighty host of the "men of Odin," prayed his last
prayer, gave all the money he had to a trusty follower for the Christian priests, "that they may pray
for the souls of mine enemies;" and then, worn out
with fatigue, fell asleep with his head in his foster-
brother's lap, to be suddenly aroused by the roar
of the onrushing swarm of destroyers.

Then he told of the fight itself—how, in the very
height of it, the sun hid his face, and all was dark,
and still the slaughter went on, "every man doing
such work as he might for the darkness;" how,
twice over, the prowess of Olaf and his handful
of heroes all but turned the day against the overwhelming host of the heathen; and how, in the thick
of the fray, he came hand to hand with the wizard-
chief, Kalf Arn's son (at whose name Macduff started
visibly), and he, "on whose enchanted coat of deer-
skin no steel would bite," gave the king a mortal
wound. Down sank Olaf on a stone, and his foes
came up and slew him; and Harold himself, striving
to defend his brother, was cut down and left for
dead, and borne away secretly at nightfall by a
friendly peasant.

Then the song went on to tell his adventures after
his flight from Norway with a handful of followers—
how he scoured the coasts of Denmark and Sweden;

how he fought for his life with Jomsburg pirates,
Lett savages, Wendish heathens, and Danish sea-
kings; how he at last landed in "Muscovy," and
penetrated as far as Great Novgorod, where he
became a prime favourite with prince and people;
and how, on a voyage to the Orkneys, he had been
caught by a storm that drove him down the east
coast of Scotland to the mouth of the Frith of Forth,
and left him no choice but to run right into it, and
take his chance of being slain by the natives.

Then he frankly avowed his meditated storming
of Macduff's castle, at which the thane laughed
good-humouredly; such a thing being too much a
matter of course in those days for any one to take
offence at it. He touched lightly on the wolf fight
and the rescue of Kenneth, and then wound up with
the suggestion for which the eager boy had listened
anxiously from the first,—

> "Chieftain of Scotland,
>   Thy son sits beside me,
>   His place is with warriors,
>   Where warriors should be ;
>   A brave lad, a true lad,
>   A lad full of mettle,
>   Deep bites the wolf's tooth,
>   More deep thy son's spearhead ;
>   Give him armour and weapons,
>   And forth let him venture,
>   And over the swan's bath
>   Go sailing with me ! "

A shout that made the hall ring applauded Prince Harold as he ended. To all who heard it, the concluding offer seemed a very fit and graceful mode of showing his sense of the thane's kindness; and even Kenneth's mother, though she shrank a little from the idea of parting with her boy so soon, felt that such an offer, made by the most famous captain of the age, was not to be lightly refused.

Then spoke Macduff himself, with a side glance at the glowing face of his eager son,—

"Harold of Norway! thou hast sung well and spoken well. Better comrade than thee could I never find for this lad of mine, and right gladly would I let him sail with thee; but I too have somewhat to tell. On my way hither I was met by a bode [messenger] from King Donacha [Duncan]—"

All the listeners pricked up their ears, already guessing what was to come.

"He brought word," went on the thane, "that I must hasten straightway, with all the men I can muster, to join the king beyond the Tay, for the Danes are on our coast once more!"

Again the hall echoed with a shout that shook the soot in flakes from the blackened rafters.

"A westerly gale drove them off the shore ere they could land," pursued Macduff, "but this wind that now bloweth will assuredly bring them back again; and certain prisoners taken in one of their ships that was wrecked by the storm told that what with Danes and Norsemen and Jomsburgers, their host is many thousands strong, and led by a chief of great might, one Kalf Arn's son."

At that name Prince Harold gave a start, and his bright, handsome young face was darkened by a frown as black as a thunder-cloud, which no one who had heard his song was at a loss to interpret.

"Now," ended the thane, "when the king calls, and our land is in peril, and my clansmen march with me to war, I ween it is not meet that my son's place in our array should be empty."

"Nor shall it!" cried Harold vehemently; "nor shall my place by his side be empty either. Hear me, chief of the Scots. If thou thinkst that thou owest me aught for what I have done this day, let me and my men go with thee, and set me in the fore-front of the fight, where I may likeliest meet with Kalf the wizard, who slew my brother!"

"As thou sayest, so be it," said Macduff heartily; "and blithe will we be, I trow, to have with us such warriors as ye be, for well saith the old rede, 'Bare is back without brother behind.' This night, then, let us be merry; on the morrow we march northward."

CHAPTER V.

A PROPHETIC DREAM.

THAT very night Macduff's messengers were speeding off on every side; and the rising sun glittered on a bristling forest of spears, axes, short swords, and spiked clubs all around the castle, which, as Harold of Norway feelingly said, "warmed his very heart to look at."

Others kept coming in all through the morning; and when, about midday, Macduff, leaving one or two of the lesser chiefs to bring up the rest, set off on his march northward, he went forth with several hundred stout fellows at his back, not counting the forty recruits (themselves worth a whole army) brought him by Prince Harold.

Away, away over the bleak Fife moors, still swept by the howling gale, past the dark waters of Loch Leven and its lonely rock islet, not yet crowned with the historical castle that Sir Walter Scott's genius has made so famous, and over the Ochil Hills down into Strathearn.

Still pressing on, they looked admiringly (at least Prince Harold did) at the " bones of the elder world " starting up around the future site of Dunkeld, crossed the Tay ferry—unwarned by any foreboding of the terrible day which was to stamp that spot in Macduff's memory for ever—and plunged into the heart of that wild region which, as late as the time of George II., a French geographer could set down on a new map as " barren wilds inhabited by savage *Hig*-landers."

During the whole of this march, which went on night and day, with just enough rest to keep the men from breaking down, Kenneth and Harold were inseparable ; and the young sea-king took as much pains to ensure his adopted brother making a good figure in his first battle as a chaperon of our day might take to prepare a young lady for being presented at court.

" Thy men will look to thee to show thyself a man, brother Kenneth," said he ; " and so must thou do, being the son of their chief. But have no care about that, for I will be ever at thy side, and guide thee where there is the most danger."

" I thank thee, brother Harold," simply replied the boy, to whom, as to any one in that age, this avowed purpose to ram him into all possible perils seemed the height of courtesy ; " but why do we halt so suddenly ? "

" Because we can go no farther, son of our chief," growled a hard-faced old clansman just in front of him.

One glance told the friends that it was but too true.

Right before them yawned a black and hideous chasm, at least a hundred feet in depth, over which there was no passing, the rude log-bridge that had once spanned it having either fallen or been hurled into the abyss.

" Evil betide the dolt who built yon bridge so ill ! " cried Macduff fiercely ; " now must we go round a good league and more, and lose time just when we need it most."

" Nay, why so ? " said Prince Harold lightly. " There are trees in plenty on the other side, and one of them, or two at the most, will make bridge enow for us all."

" But how to reach them ? " angrily retorted the thane, provoked, as he might well be, by what seemed to him a mere ill-timed jest.

" Leap across," replied the young sea-king quietly.

And ere any one could speak or move he had flung down his steel cap and battle-axe, and drawing

himself together like a lion about to spring, flew at
the desperate leap.

It *was* a desperate leap indeed—fully seventeen
feet from lip to lip of the chasm; and all alike gave
a quick gasp as they saw him shoot out into the
empty air, while even his own men turned away
their faces. But a lusty shout made them look round
again to see him standing safe on the other side.

"Fling me over mine axe, thane," cried he cheerily
to the amazed Macduff, "and thou shalt soon see a
clear path before thee."

It was done, and instantly the young giant's axe
fell like a thunderbolt on one of the two pines that
grew side by side close to the brink; and stroke
followed stroke, the chips flying up at every blow
like a shower of spray.

Already the trunk was beginning to crack and
quiver, when Harold, fastening both hands on it,
threw into one mighty heave the full power of a
strength one day to be proverbial from the Gulf of
Finland to the Atlantic. Crash! down came the
stately pine right across the chasm; and in a few
minutes more the other lay beside it, and Macduff's
men were streaming over this impromptu bridge, with
a shout of "Hail to the sea-king! Hail to the
strongest of the Norsemen!"

"It must be a goodly thing to feel that one hath such strength as thine!" cried Kenneth, looking up admiringly at the young Hercules by his side as they moved on again.

"As to that," said Harold, who seemed to think little of the feat when once achieved, "it is the spirit, not the body, that gives might to a warrior; and he whose heart is strong is a match for giants, even as King David of old."

Northward, northward ever, struggling up ridge after ridge of steep pine-clad hills, splashing across pebbly torrent-beds, crashing through tangled thickets, winding in single file between the jutting crags of vast black overhanging precipices, or leaping from tussock to tussock of treacherous morasses, till at last the great dark wall of the Grampian mountains lay behind them, and from its northern slope they looked down the far-extending sweep of Strathspey, and beheld the endless windings of its famous river glittering along the wide green valley like a silver thread in the glory of the morning sunlight.

But the stillness that brooded over that marvellous panorama, deep and solemn as the silence of a newly-created world, was broken all at once by a clash of steel far below, and a hoarse clamour of conflicting shouts.

"What now?" cried Macduff, throwing up his head like a deerhound scenting game; "can these Danish ravens have flown so far inland already? Well, if it be so, we are ready for them. Forward!"

But his men needed no urging. Down the hillside they rushed pell-mell, right toward the spot whence the noise seemed to proceed.

But when they got past the thickets that fringed the lower slopes, an unlooked-for sight met their eyes. Two small bodies of men were contending in the valley below, and one of the two was visibly getting the worst of it; but by their dress and equipment both sides appeared to be Scots. What could this mean?

The first idea of the lookers-on (a very natural one in that age) was that two Scottish chiefs, betwixt whom lay some cause of quarrel, had met on their way to repel the Danish invader, and had at once set to work to slay each other in place of the common enemy.

But all this mattered little to Macduff and his men. In that warlike age the first thought of any man who found a fight going on (no matter about what or between whom) was to join in at once; and forward hurried one and all to do so.

Just then came a sudden lull in the battle, and

both sides fell back a little so as to leave an open space, in the midst of which two men stood front to front; and the Fife men guessed at once that, as often happened in those days, the combatants were suspending their own conflict to let their leaders try each other's strength.

At it went the two champions like giants, the one with an axe, the other with a sword; and so thick and fast fell their blows that the eye could hardly follow them. At first the fight seemed equal, but ere long the axeman was seen to be failing; his strokes grew fainter, his strength flagged, and it was plain that he was overmatched.

Driven to desperation as he felt himself giving way, he made a last effort, and, springing forward, whirled up his weapon for a decisive blow. But ere the axe could fall the other darted in under it; there was a flash of steel, a hoarse cry, and then, as the whirling dust subsided, the one champion was seen lying motionless at the other's feet.

Dismayed by their leader's fall, some of his followers threw down their arms and asked mercy, while others broke and fled, hotly pursued by the conqueror's men.

"Who is yon chief who hath so stoutly overcome his foe?" asked Harold of his friend Kenneth; for

by this time their advance had brought them so close
to the scene of action that every face in it could be
plainly seen.

"Thane Macbeth," said the boy, little foreseeing
the gloomy and terrible renown which that name
was to attain ages after its owner's death. "He
leads the men of Cromarty to war, and we account
him our best warrior—after my father," added he
quickly.

"He is a goodly man and a stout champion," said
the young sea-king, with an approving glance at
Macbeth's tall, sinewy form and handsome though
rather stern face, framed in shaggy, dark-red hair.
"Howbeit," he added gravely, "there is somewhat in
his face that mislikes me, I wot not why."

Kenneth looked surprised; but ere he could speak,
Macbeth's keen gray eye caught sight of the Fife
banner floating over the advancing force, and forward he hastened to greet his old friend and fellow-
thane, Macduff.

But hardly had they time to exchange greetings
when the blast of a war-horn came echoing along the
valley; and Macbeth, not knowing who the newcomers might be, lost no time in blowing his own
horn to recall his men from the pursuit, while the
rest of his followers, joining the men of Fife, drew

up across the battlefield in readiness for whatever might befall.

But it was a friendly banner, as Macbeth soon saw, that waved over the coming band; and well did he know the square, sturdy form that issued with extended hand from the mass of armed men and came toward him, clad in a finely-wrought coat of mail and a silver-crested helmet, and showing in every movement the strength and agility of a practised warrior in spite of the slight lameness which, attending him from his birth, had given him the name of " Baccogh " (lame).

" It is the Thane of Lochaber, Macbeth's cousin, and a warrior of renown," said Kenneth to Harold, as they stood watching the meeting.

" Welcome, noble cousin; I am right glad to meet thee again," cried Baccogh of Lochaber, warmly grasping Macbeth's hand. " Hast thou had tidings from home since thy departure, or am I the first to bring them ? "

" No ill news, I trust ? " said Macbeth anxiously; " my father, when I departed, seemed to be mending of his sickness."

" He is dead," said the other gravely; " and thou art Thane of Cromarty in his stead."

Macbeth gave a slight start, and mingling with his

natural grief came a strange look of surprise, not wholly untinged with awe.

"The same messenger who gave us the news," went on his cousin, "brought word that the false Thane of Moray, who, as thou knowest, is thought to have called hither the Danish fleet from the Orkneys, had openly turned traitor, and set forth with all his men to join the invader. So the king sent me out with these stout lads of mine to meet and fall upon the treacherous rogue by the way; but meseems," he added, with a glance at the trampled banner and the dead who lay around it, "that thou hast thyself taken the job out of my hand."

"Even so," said Macbeth grimly, as he pointed to the fallen chief at his feet: "here lies the Thane of Moray, never to play the traitor more. May God have mercy on his soul!"

"Ha!" cried Baccogh, "hath he fallen by thy hand? Nay, then, cousin, I have to greet thee with yet another title. King Duncan said, in the hearing of all our chiefs, that yon dead traitor had forfeited his rank by his treason, and that he who slew him should be Thane of Moray in his stead. Hail to thee, cousin, Thane of Cromarty and Moray!"

Again Macbeth started, and the look of awe-stricken amazement deepened visibly on his bold, handsome face.

" What they said was true, then, in very deed," he muttered hoarsely.

" What they said ? " echoed his friend, looking surprised. " Why, hath any one told thee this already ? I have come straight to thee from the king with the news."

Macbeth seemed hardly to hear him, and stood silent for a moment or two as if in deep thought.

" Cousin Baccogh," said he at last, " I have a strange tale to tell thee, but thou knowest that it is not my wont to lie. Know, then, that as I took a brief slumber on our march hither from the west I dreamed a dream. Up rose before me, as it seemed, on the bare moor, as if they had sprung from the earth, three women, taller and fairer than any of mortal race ; and the first greeted me as Thane of Cromarty, and the second as Thane of Moray ! " *

By this time his cousin's face was quite as grave as his own, for in those days all men alike believed firmly in dreams ; and, in truth, the speedy and

---

* Such, according to the most ancient traditions, was the real fact so magnificently expanded by Shakespeare in his conception of the " three weird sisters." Macbeth's real title was Thane of Cromarty, and the oldest authorities call the traitor not Thane of Cawdor, but Thane of Moray.

literal fulfilment of this strange prophecy would have
been startling even to a far less credulous age.

"And the third," asked Baccogh eagerly; "did
the third say naught to thee?"

For an instant Macbeth hesitated; and then he
replied with sombre emphasis,—

"The third wore the form and face of Dame
Graoch, mine own wife; and thus said she to me,
'Yet a little while, and men shall hail thee as King
of the Scots!'"

"Said she so?" cried the Thane of Lochaber
excitedly. "Nay, then, since two of the bodings
have come to pass, who can say if the third too may
not yet be fulfilled in its turn? There be many
men, as thou knowest, who deem that thou hast
a better right to the title of King of the Scots than
he who now beareth it, though ye be both of you the
grandsons of King Malcolm II.; and if—"

"Hold thy peace!" broke in Macbeth, with a sudden fierceness that startled even his stolid kinsman.
"What boots it to stand prating of such matters
when war is at our very doors? Close up, and let
us on with all speed to join the king's host, and to
scare these Danish ravens from their prey!"

CHAPTER VI.

THE STORM OF STEEL.

WHILE the two leaders were thus talking apart, the men of Cromarty and Fife mingled familiarly with those of Lochaber, among whom Kenneth Macduff espied a lad about his own age, who, the moment he caught sight of our hero, ran to him and seized him by the hand with a gleeful shout of welcome.

"Well met, Fillan-na-Nish!" (Fillan of the Point), cried Kenneth heartily. "I am blithe to see thee once more. What? thou art come, then, even as I, to have thy first taste of the storm of steel at thy father's side?"

"Ay, truly, comrade Kenneth," said the boy. "When our land is in peril, and the foe is on her shore with fire and sword, I trow it is no time for any one who can wield a weapon to sit idle at home; wherefore I craved leave of my father to strike a blow for Scotland under the banner of the clan."

While his friend was speaking, Macduff had been
looking hard at a tall, handsome young man in the
Lochaber ranks, who was conspicuous not only by
his height and strength, but also by the fashion of
his armour; for his helmet had the long, projecting
"nose-piece" of the Saxon, and the huge battle-axe
on his shoulder was of the double-bladed Saxon kind
known as a twy-bill.

"Who is yon young champion," asked the lad,
"who seemeth by the fashion of his dress to be a
Southron?"

"A Southron he is, in very deed. It is Asbiorn,
the son of the great Earl Siward the Stout of Northumbria, come hither to visit our king."

"And he hath good luck to have come now,
just in time to take a hand in our sword-play with
these Danish thieves."

"He will do good work, too, for men say he is a
famous warrior already; but ofttimes it well-nigh
makes me laugh to hear how his Saxon tongue stum-
bleth at these northern names of ours. My father,
Baccogh, he ever calls Banquo; and of my name,
Fillan-na-Nish, he can make naught but Fleance.
What thinkest thou of that?"

And the two boys laughed heartily at these
blunders, little guessing that those mispronounced

names were to be famed through the whole world, long after the real ones were utterly forgotten.

It was at that moment that Macbeth gave his cousin the signal to resume the march; and Baccogh, leading forward the young Saxon, said heartily,—

"Cousin Macbeth, I bring thee here an approved champion, Earl Siward's son Asbiorn, than whom no better warrior marches in our host."

Asbiorn (Bear of the Gods), whose name yet lives in our English "Osborne," exchanged a cordial greeting with Macbeth, unwarned by any foreboding that the hand which grasped his own so warmly was one day to take his life; for Shakespeare's "young Siward," who also fell at Dunsinane, was not the great earl's son, but his nephew.

Then Macduff stepped forward in his turn, and said to the other two leaders,—

"I, too, fellow-thanes, have brought a champion with me, whose name needs neither skald [poet] nor herald to make it known; for who has not heard of the deeds of Harold, Sigurd's son, of Norway?"

At that renowned name an admiring murmur, swelling by degrees into a lusty shout of applause, billowed through the ranks of the Lochaber and Cromarty men; and Kenneth felt his heart leap at the thought that this mighty hero, whose very name

could kindle such enthusiasm, was his own adopted
brother, under whose guidance he might himself
grow into a famous chief, and a staunch defender of
his native land.

Down this open valley their march went on more
easily than amid the rocky hills and pathless thickets
through which they had been struggling so long, and
it was still early in the afternoon when they reached
the royal camp, and were heartily welcomed by King
Duncan himself; not the mild, venerable, white-
haired old man imaged by Shakespeare, but a stalwart Scottish warrior of middle age, whose hard face,
framed in grayish-yellow hair, looked very much like
a granite block overgrown with lichens, and whose
bare arms—for he was as roughly dressed as any
of his men—showed the scars of many a hard
battle.

By the king's side stood his eldest son, Malcolm,
who was just placing his dinted helmet on the broad,
high brow of that massive head which gave him his
now historical nickname of " Canmore," or Great
Head ; and around the two were grouped a number
of chiefs, whose shout of welcome at the arrival of
their two greatest captains was repeated with double
energy as soon as they heard that the young golden-
haired giant at Macduff's side was no other than

Prince Harold, Sigurd's son, of Norway, and that the traitor Thane of Moray had already got his due.

Then King Duncan and his chiefs held a hasty council of war.

The Danes had not yet landed, but their ships had been seen again, in no small number, off the Elgin coast. Somewhere on that strip of shore they would land, beyond a doubt; but where?

At Lossiemouth, said the king and many of his chiefs; at Findhorn Loch, farther to the west, said Macbeth and his cousin Baccogh, who urged, with some show of reason, that the invaders, knowing nothing of the treacherous Thane of Moray's defeat and death, would, of course, come as far west as they could, in order to join him at once.

Each side clung to its own opinion—neither was willing to yield—and meanwhile time was passing, and every moment precious.

Then stood forward Prince Harold, and said modestly,—

"It is not for my youth to counsel older warriors and wiser men; but methinks this matter is easily settled. Let the king go to Lossiemouth, and Thane Macbeth to Findhorn Loch; and as the two hosts will not be far apart, let whichever first espies the Danes send a swift messenger to warn the other, that so these Danish wolves may have one host in front to fight them, and the other behind to cut them off from their ships."

This plan struck every man who heard it as a very good idea, and, as usual in such cases, they all wondered that no one had thought of it before. The king agreed to it there and then, and marched at once towards Lossiemouth with his own force, while Macbeth, Baccogh, and Macduff headed down the valley towards the town of Forres and the mouth of the Findhorn river.

With the king went young Asbiorn; but Harold, to Kenneth's great joy, decided to stay with the Fife men, and to fight under the banner of Macduff.

Night came down upon them ere long—a gloomy, stormy, moonless March night; but on they went still, for who could tell whether the Danes might not now be burning and murdering within a few miles of them?

But at last it grew so utterly dark that they were forced to halt whether they would or no, for fear of walking right down a precipice, or plunging headlong into the rushing river beside them. Then Macbeth bade his men lie down and sleep while they could; for himself, he said, he would keep watch; and Harold offered to watch with him, while Macduff and Baccogh slept.

But the gloom was not long unbroken. All at once, far in front of them, a fierce red glare burst through the engulfing blackness, mounting ever higher and higher, till the whole sky seemed ablaze.

Beneath that infernal splendour the rushing stream of the Divie Water appeared to run blood. The dark rocks and tall pine-stems glowed as if red-hot, and the grim, bearded faces of the Scottish warriors, as they started from their broken sleep, came and went like phantoms, with a fleck of deep, gory red on every spear and helmet, as if already dyed with the coming slaughter.

"Yon beacon light tells its own tale," said Macbeth with a stern smile; "we need no further warning. —Ha! who comes here?"

There was a rush of hurrying steps, and a man, all but running against him, stumbled and fell sprawling at his feet.

"Ye be Scots, thank God!" said the newcomer gaspingly. "Make speed to aid us, as ye are men."

"That will we," said Macbeth, helping him up. "Speak quickly; where have the Danes landed?"

"At Findhorn Loch," panted the other, "and they have sacked the abbey and Forres town, and set them both on fire; and many huts have they burned, mine own among the rest. A plague on them for it! it had not been burned since summer—"

Here his voice failed, and he sank heavily forward, as if fainting; and by the glare of the flames Macbeth saw that his face was bleeding freely, and that one arm hung helplessly at his side.

"We must send word to the king at once," cried the thane, as he tore a strip from his own plaid and hastily bound up the messenger's hurts.

"That shall be my charge," broke in Harold. "Where is Biorn Hare-foot?"

"At thy shoulder, prince, as ever," said a deep voice behind him.

"Hie thee, Biorn! thou know'st which way the king hath gone; run as a deer with the wolves behind it, and bid him slip between the Danes and their ships. Go, lad, and God speed thee!"

The words were answered by a heavy plunge in the water below; and a few moments later came a cheery shout from the other side of the river, and then the quick pit-pat of the runner's feet dying away gradually in the gloom beyond.

"And now," cried Baccogh eagerly, "let us forward at once, and pounce upon these sea-wolves in the midst of their meal."

But Macbeth, who, as he showed in after days,

was a general as well as a fighting man, promptly checked his cousin's rash ardour.

" Be not hasty, kinsman ; this task craves wary walking. Could we have come upon them in the dark, all had been well ; but by this blaze they can see us a league off, and we must deal warily."

And then he called up one of his trustiest followers, and gave him some brief, clear directions.

He was to go to the Danes as if coming from the traitor Thane of Moray, whose arrival to aid them, with all his men, the invaders were hourly expecting, little dreaming that he had already paid the penalty of his treason. He was to tell them that when they should see armed men coming down the valley they must hasten forward and join them ; and then he was to vanish at once, awaiting no further question.

Away went the bold envoy, knowing well that these wild rovers, already hot with slaughter, might very possibly kill him ere he could tell his errand ; but he never hesitated a whit for that.

Meanwhile the three thanes and their forces went slowly on down the valley, right towards the blaze that was kindling earth and sky ; and as they advanced they began to hear faintly, borne to them on the night wind, fierce shouts, savage yells, and wild shrieks for aid, at which the Scots set their teeth grimly, and clutched their spears and axe-shafts as if they would break them.

"Would that we could have joined battle at once! it is weary work, this waiting," said Kenneth, who, like all young soldiers, was eager to begin, and found the suspense before the fight by far the hardest trial of all.

"Even so felt I in my first battle," said his friend Prince Harold quietly, with a knowing smile. "While we stood waiting, every minute seemed as long as an hour; and when the word was given to fall on, it was as if a great stone were rolled from off my heart. But patience, lad; thou wilt have thy fill anon."

In fact, their envoy came back in a surprisingly short time (though to the impatient Kenneth it seemed an age) to report that his device had been quite successful; that the Danes were fully prepared to welcome as friends any men whom they might meet coming from that quarter; and that, moreover, the greater part of the invaders had dispersed over the face of the country in quest of fresh booty, and not a few of them (as Macbeth's experience had shrewdly foreseen) were already helplessly stupefied with the liquor found in the plundered town.

A mile more, and the ever-widening valley had

opened on to the vast expanse of bare moor lying to the south of Forres, now lighted up far and wide with the glare of the distant flames.

Here, so far from making any attempt to hide their presence, the Scots spread out to right and left as widely as they could, and kept shouting the Moray war-cry with the full might of their powerful voices.

This drew, as it was meant to do, the attention of all the Danes within hearing; and ere long a straggling swarm of shadowy figures could be seen hurrying towards them over the dark moor. The Scots waited till the newcomers were all but upon them, and then, with a mighty shout, they rushed on the startled and unprepared robbers, and the harvest of death began.

It is always hard for an untried man to guess how he will feel in his first battle; and, as a rule, it turns out to be quite different from what he had expected. Kenneth Macduff was dimly conscious of a whirl of grim faces and wild forms and flashing weapons all around him, coming and going like the phantoms of a dream—of parrying and returning thrusts and blows—of adding his own shouts to the terrific din that seemed to shake the very earth; and then, all at once, came a dead silence, and the cloud of tossing arms and furious faces vanished, and

the boy found himself supported by the strong arm
of Prince Harold, while beside him stood his friend
Fillan, Baccogh's son, whose gashed brow and dinted
armour told that he too had been in the thick of
the fray.

"Not sore hurt, I hope, brother Kenneth," said
the young sea-king cheerily.

"*Am* I hurt?" asked the lad, waking as if from
a dream.

"Thou bleedst as if thou wert," laughed the
Norseman, to whom any hurt that did not actually
kill a man was a mere joke, as he bound up the
boy's wounded arm. "Sit thee down here, for thou
wilt be sick and faint ere long, and—"

But here he broke off, and, springing up, flew like
a deerhound to the other side of the battlefield.

The first body of Danes, outnumbered and taken
by surprise, had been swept away like dust; and the
same lot fell to a band of Orkney men who came
up to aid them. But the alarm had spread, and the
raiders were now flocking from all sides to repel the
attack; and among them came a band of picked
Norse warriors, in which Hårold's keen eye singled
out Kalf Arn's son, the "wizard chief" who had
slain his brother!

In an age when discipline was not, and when

every " army " was a mere armed mob, and every battle a series of single combats, most of the leading champions on either side, as in the days of Homer, knew each other by sight, and were wont to exchange rough " chaff " ere closing in mortal combat.

" Kalf Arn's son ! " shouted Harold at the full pitch of his mighty voice.

The " wizard " stepped boldly forward ; but as he knew the towering form that confronted him, his face changed.

" Harold Sigurd's son ? I thought thee dead. Hast thou then arisen from the grave ? "

" No," said Harold sternly ; " God hath saved me from death to punish thee. Thou shalt die by my hand, as my brother died by thine ! "

" He trusted in the ' White Christ,' and I in Odin," said the heathen chief, " and I proved the stronger. How if we try it again now ? "

" So be it," cried Harold ; " we fight, then—thou for Odin, and I for Christ."

Little thought the fiery young chief with what weapons He whose champion he claimed to be had conquered the whole world. To the fierce northern warriors—" the people who delighted in war "—the creed that bade them love their enemies was always a puzzling mystery, and ages had to pass ere they learned that the only power which could overcome them was "the irresistible might of weakness."

To it they went like giants; but so quick was Kalf's eye, and so agile his spring, that his foe's terrific blows were wasted on the empty air, or, as Harold's native superstition suggested, turned by the wizard's enchanted coat.

"With such magic didst thou overcome my brother but let us see if any magic is proof against a strong arm!" cried he; and dropping his axe, he rushed in and seized his foe in a hug that might have crushed a Norway bear.

Once in that terrible clutch Kalf, strong as he was, had no more chance than an ox in the coils of a boa; and in a moment he was swung off his feet, and dashed to the earth with a force that left him stunned and helpless, with his sword-arm lying broken beneath him.

Harold delayed the final blow, for his heart warmed to the gallant foe who lay powerless at his feet; but he knew how vain it was to offer mercy to one who would have died by his own hand rather than survive the shame of being vanquished by a boy.

"Strike! I ask no mercy!" cried the fallen man, looking up unquailingly at the fatal axe that glittered over his head.

"I have won the game, in truth," said Harold; "but hast thou no boon to ask ere thou diest? Be it what it may, I will grant it."

"I thank thee," gasped the sufferer, "nor do I bear thee any grudge; thou hast but done what I would have done to thee. Bury me, then, with my weapons and armour, and let no hand but thine lay me in my grave, for thou art a great warrior. Now strike!"

"Hold!" cried Harold; "I would not kill both body and soul. Thou seest that Christ is stronger than Odin; wilt thou not yield thyself to Him ere it be too late?"

"Ay; He is the stronger," said the doomed man faintly, "and had I lived I would have been His man. Strike, lad!"

Harold's axe flashed and fell, and with it fell a brave man's life.

CHAPTER VII.

A ROYAL DINNER-PARTY.

JOVIAL was the feasting and loud the revelry in the camp pitched by King Duncan beside the ruins of the burned abbey, on the night after the victory over the Danish marauders; and, in truth, that victory was worthy to be celebrated, for it had been far more complete than the most hopeful had dared to expect.

Disheartened by the loss of their great leader, Kalf Arn's son, and by the fall of two other chiefs whom Macbeth and his cousin had struck down, the Danes were already beginning to give ground, when the king and his army, warned by Biorn Hare-foot, fell upon them from the other side, and cut them off from their ships. Then all gave way. Some turned fiercely to bay, and died fighting to the last; others fled, and were cut down in their flight; and not a few perished in the lake, or in trying to swim the flooded Findhorn.

The very elements seemed to fight for Scotland; for the Danish fleet, like that of King Hakon at Largs two centuries later, was caught in a storm ere it could clear the land, and many of the vessels were driven ashore, ships and crews perishing together. In short, it was but a mere remnant of the ill-fated host that escaped that great harvest of death; and for many a year to come the boldest rovers of the north were very chary of venturing another descent on the fatal coast that had devoured so many of their best and bravest.

A strange scene it was that midnight banquet on the battlefield, lit up by the fitful glare of the camp fires and the cold splendour of the rising moon. King Duncan's canopy was the starlit sky, his carpet the heather of the moor, on which he and his chief thanes sat together amid the corpses of their foes, with their hands and faces still red with recent slaughter, hacking their meat with the same weapons that had just been hewing down the Danes, gnawing the bones clean, and then flinging them on the ground or at their neighbours, as the fancy happened to take them.

At the first glance a stranger would have found it no easy matter to tell the king from any other of the wild, shaggy-haired, bare-armed forms around him;

nor, in truth, was there much difference, real or apparent. Each of these powerful chiefs was a kind of king in his way, and quite as great a man —in his own opinion, at least—as the king himself, to whom he was always ready to speak his mind freely, and to follow up his words with blows if they happened to be ill received.

"Who is yon dame who sits by Thane Macbeth's side?" asked Prince Harold of his next neighbour, the elder Macduff.

"His wife, Dame Graoch," said Macduff, "who came up this day, toward the end of the fight, with a band of fresh men that she had gathered just in time to give these Danish wolves one more taste of Scottish steel as they fled."

"It was boldly done, and in truth she is a goodly dame, but I like her not," said Harold, with mediæval frankness. "Meseems she hath the air of one of the witch-wives of whom our northern stories tell, who could sink ships with their spells, and take away in battle, by magic, the might of kings and champions, and lure men to ruin with the sound of their enchanted song. Thou knowest the old ballad, belike,—

'I've heard that with the witches' song, tho' harsh and rude it be,
There blends a wild, mysterious strain of weirdest harmony;
So that the list'ner far away must needs approach the ring
Where, on the savage Lapland moor, the demon chorus sing.'"

At that moment King Duncan rose to his feet, and holding up a brimming horn, called out,—

" Health to Harold, Sigurd's son, the sea-king, who hath this day done best of us all, and hath won us a victory that shall be sung of and spoken of long after the 'four stones' are set on our graves ! "

Though the king spoke so courteously, it was plain to all that he was most royally out of temper ; and, in truth, not without cause. Eager as he was, like all kings of that age, to stand first in warlike renown among his people, the consciousness of having gone off on a false scent, and had no part in the fight save following up a success already won for him by the valour of other men, stung him to the quick.

" Thou givest me more than my due, king," said the Norse hero modestly, in reply to Duncan's toast. " I did what I could, but he to whom ye owe the victory is the valiant thane Macbeth, who hath indeed done better than all."

Duncan winced, and his dark brow grew darker yet at the applauding murmur that followed. He knew well that, as Baccogh had said, there were many who held Macbeth's title to the crown to be as good as, if not better than, his own ; and though outwardly friendly, there was no love lost between them.

"It is much to say that he hath done better than all," said he sourly; "I grant that he hath done as well as some."

"Wilt thou bear that and yet call thyself a man?" hissed Dame Graoch in Macbeth's ear.

The great leader answered never a word; but he clenched his strong right hand till the knuckles grew white, and with a mighty effort choked down his rising wrath.

But his cousin Baccogh, less master of himself, resented, like a true Scot, his kinsman's wrong as if it had been his own, and turning fiercely on Duncan, said with a bitter emphasis that cut like a whip,—

"Thou art right, king: he hath done as well as some who held back till the fight was won, and then came up for the gleaning of Macbeth's harvest!"

Had Duncan requited this open affront by killing the insulter on the spot, no one would have been surprised; for in that rough age it was quite a common thing for some turbulent noble to insult the king to his face, and for the king to strike him dead in return. But Duncan masked his growing fury with a show of utter scorn, and said with cold contempt,—

"I spake to Macbeth, not to thee. Meek is

Macbeth, in sooth, if he dares not reply for himself, but lets his gillie [servant] speak for him."

But for Macbeth's restraining grasp his fiery
cousin would have flung himself upon the king
there and then; and Graoch, with a look of
deadly hatred at the unconscious Duncan, whispered
to her husband,—

" Yonder sits the man whose grandsire slew my
grandsire,* whose father slew thine uncle, and who
hath himself stolen the crown that should be thine;
and now is he putting open shame on thy kinsman
and on thee, and still thou sayest naught!"

Macbeth's iron hand closed on the drink-horn that
he held with such terrific force that the horn cracked
and split like glass, and fell in shivers at his feet;
but his set face never changed a whit.

" Hush thee, housewife," said he, with a stern
calmness more ominous than the loudest anger;
" thou wilt not cure a raw wound by pricking
it with a bodkin, and other than bodkin stabs are
needed here!"

Then he rose slowly to his feet, and said, with a
nameless something in his look and tone that awed
the boldest of those who heard him,—

* Such, according to the best authorities, was Lady Macbeth's
real cause of quarrel with Duncan—an amply sufficient one in a
land of hereditary feuds such as Scotland.

" King Duncan, I have been 'meek,' as thou sayest, too long already ; and what I dare, thou shalt shortly learn.   Farewell ! when we meet again, thou wilt be more blithe of our parting than of our meeting."

And with that ominous warning—which has since passed into a proverb—the great leader turned his back on the startled king and, followed by his wife and cousin and by most of his friends, slowly withdrew.

CHAPTER VIII.

WHAT BEFELL AT THE "SMITH'S HOUSE."

IN an age when every man believed in the existence of ghosts, witches, and supernatural beings of every kind as firmly as he believed in his own, the wild region of northern Scotland naturally abounded in "haunted spots." But of all these there was not one more dreaded, or more carefully shunned after dark by the boldest of the country folk, than a spot not far from the town of Elgin, popularly known as "Both-Gowan" (the smith's house).

Just where the last spurs of the great mountain range melted into the wide sweep of bare moorland that stretched right up to the bleak shore of the northern sea, stood in a deep, gloomy hollow, between two dark wooded ridges, a great heap of slab-like boulders of moss-clad granite, piled one on the other in such a way as to bear a rude likeness to a small stone hut. In front of it lay a broad flat stone, such as one sees in the "Druid circles" of southern

England, Guernsey, and Brittany, on which—as the local peasants whispered with awe-stricken looks—any one who dared to pass the dreaded spot at night would hear the ceaseless strokes of a smith's hammer, though nothing was to be seen.

The explanations of this marvel given by the peasantry, as with the similar legend of "Wayland Smith" in Berkshire, were many and various.

Some averred this ghostly artisan to be the troubled spirit of a local smith of great fame, who, having been so rash as to work on a Sunday or a saint's day in defiance of all warning, was doomed to suffer for his impiety by working there till the end of time. Others declared that the mysterious smith was one of the underground dwarfs so famous in northern legends, who, being, as every one knew, imprisoned all day in the depths of the earth, and only allowed to come up at night, were wont to avenge these restrictions by doing all the harm they could to any ill-starred mortal who fell in their way. As these dwarfs were held to be the best smiths in the world, the ascribing of this midnight hammering to them was natural enough.

There were three or four versions of this weird tale, each more startling than the last; but all alike agreed in maintaining that some terrible fate was in store for any one who dared to disturb the invisible smith at his task. And fearful tales were whispered of rash intruders who, recklessly visiting the fatal spot after nightfall, had never been seen or heard of more; having been, it was supposed, either killed by the angry spirit or imprisoned for ever beneath the earth.

Even in broad daylight this ill-omened place was seldom visited; and thus the bare-limbed woodcutter who, on the second evening after the Danes' over-throw, came forth with a huge fagot on his back from the thickets of one of the flanking ridges, about half a mile from the dreaded hollow, might well be surprised to hear the silence suddenly broken by the blast of a war-horn, and to see a straggling line of spears and helmets come glittering down the valley right toward the haunted dell.

"These, I trow," muttered the woodman, "are some of yon warriors who, two days since, overthrew the Danish robbers; and now, in the pride of their victory, they must needs march past this place of evil, as if there were no other way for them to go! Well for them if the old saying prove not true, 'High heart brings low fall!'"

But even as he spoke the man drew back into

the bushes till he was quite hidden; for a sudden glimpse of the banner that waved over the coming band told him that their leader was no other than King Duncan himself. The memory of certain unpaid "forest dues" pressed heavily on the peasant's mind; and, in an age when kings and nobles were wont to collect their own taxes in a very summary way, he naturally thought it best to be on the safe side.

It was indeed the king, on his way to Elgin. His victorious army had already dispersed (as the tumultuary levies which then formed an army always did after a battle, to secure their booty if conquerors or their own safety if conquered), and he was now attended only by his personal followers.

But, as the hidden watcher could see from his lurking-place, the look and bearing of these men were not at all what might have been expected of warriors fresh from a decisive victory over their most dreaded foes. Every face was gloomy and troubled, and their words were as ominous as their looks.

"Heaven send us well out of this!" muttered one of the king's attendants to another. "It is true that we have daylight still with us, but—"

The speaker glanced down the valley toward the

haunted hollow with a look that said more than any words.

"So think I too!" growled the man to whom he spoke. "It shall never be said of me that I feared to follow the king, go where he may. But rather would I follow him through a host of Danish spears than past yon evil spot."

"There is no stopping a fey [doomed] man," said a third gloomily; "and doomed is the king, or I know naught of such matters. What think ye, brothers? When I awoke him this morn as he bade me, he looked up as one dazed, and thus he spake: 'Ah, Donald, why didst thou wake me? I dreamed that a ladder was set before me, reaching up to heaven; and I climbed up and up till my foot was on the topmost step. One moment more and I should have been there!'"

His two hearers, plainly much disturbed, exchanged looks of gloomy meaning.

"And then," went on the speaker, "I said to him, 'King, meseems thou art foredoomed; I like not yon dream of thine. Go not, I pray thee, past the smith's house this day, lest some evil befall thee.'"

"And what said the king?" asked both his comrades at once.

"He answered right fiercely, 'Doomed or no, the

way I am minded to go, go I will, and none shall turn me aside from it!'"

"It is true, there is no turning one who is doomed!" said the first man, shaking his head. "Assuredly evil is in store for him."

Hardly were the ominous words spoken when a fierce shout broke forth before, behind, and all around them, and the watching woodman above saw a crowd of armed men burst from the encircling thickets, and fall like a thunderbolt on the king and his handful of followers.

Already unnerved by superstitious fears, most of Duncan's men—hardly knowing whether they were assailed by mortal beings or by the goblins of the hollow—took to their heels at once, with cries of terror. The few who stood their ground were speedily crushed by numbers, the assailants being as two to one, and ere long the king was left almost alone.

"Stand fast, King Duncan; 'Macbeth's gillie' would try thy force," cried Baccogh of Lochaber, rushing like a lion on the man who had insulted him.

But just then a strong hand thrust him aside, and Macbeth's deep voice said in his ear,—

"Hold, cousin; this quarrel is mine.—Turn thee, king, and see if thou canst face in the field him whom thou hast scorned at the feast!"

There was a clash of steel—a confused medley of blows—a sound of heavy trampling and hard breathing—a dull thud and a deep groan—and down went King Duncan, never to rise again; while over him stood Macbeth, with a faint gleam of pity struggling through the settled sternness of his iron face as he looked down on the lifeless form that had once been his king and his friend.

"Well struck, kinsman! thou hast paid him for us both," said the Thane of Lochaber, with a grim smile, as he gazed at the fallen man.

"I have, cousin," said Macbeth; "but peace be with him, now that it is done. Not mine the blame, for it was his own act that brought this upon him; but now that he is dead, thou and I will give him such burial as befits a king and a warrior; and may God have mercy on his soul!"

Little thought the great thane, as he stood there in the triumphant consciousness of having inflicted what seemed to him a just retribution, that, ages after his death, the genius of a wool-comber's son in far-off England, from a place of which he had never heard, would rewrite the story of that day's work in words of such overwhelming power as to supersede history itself, and brand the name of Macbeth to all time with the twofold infamy of betrayed hospitality and midnight murder.

CHAPTER IX.

A RACE WITH DEATH.

SIX years had passed since that fatal evening, and the summer of 1045 was already far advanced, when, on the edge of the thick woods which then fringed the northern bank of the Tay, stood, hunting-spear in hand (as if expecting deer or wild bull to break from the cover), a tall, powerful, fair-haired young man of twenty, who, though much changed, was no other than Kenneth Macduff.

But those six years had wrought other and graver changes than the mere turning of our hero from a boy into a man.

Harold, Sigurd's son, as the chief author of Macbeth's great victory over the Danes, had been strongly urged by the great thane—when he became king by Duncan's death—to remain at the court of Scotland with all his men and enjoy the honours and rewards that he had so fully earned. But nothing could keep such a born rover from the

sea that he loved; and not long after Macbeth's
accession, Prince Harold, taking a loving farewell
of his adopted brother Kenneth, and giving him the
very spear which the young man now held, vanished
once more into the unknown, carrying with him, as
tokens of Macbeth's gratitude, "two long ships and
great store of goodly weapons therewith."

Baccogh of Lochaber and his son Fillan—the
Banquo and Fleance of Shakespeare — were
among the leading figures at Macbeth's court; and
Fillan's inseparable comrade was Kenneth Macduff,
whom Macbeth always welcomed so heartily, and
seemed so pleased to see among his courtiers, that
the warm-hearted lad naturally took a great liking
for him, having no suspicion that all this frank
kindness could mask any darker design.

The elder Macduff, as Thane of Fife, ruled his great
domain wisely and well; but the more observant
noticed that he came less and less often to Macbeth's
court, and that he seemed by no means pleased when
his son was appointed to an important post that
would keep him constantly about the king's person.

For this, however, there was but too good cause;
for the greatest and most lamentable of all the
changes wrought by those six eventful years was the
gradual alteration in Macbeth himself.

At the outset, indeed, his power, if gained by violence, was used with moderation; and, for the first three years of his reign at least, this man whom we are taught to regard as a capricious and blood-thirsty tyrant, showed himself a just and wise ruler, generous and even humane when judged by the standard of his own age.

But it seemed as if the curse of Duncan's blood, shed in fair fight though it was, still clung to its slayer.

Little by little Macbeth's once frank and noble nature was darkened by causeless and ever-growing suspicions, ceaselessly deepened by the baneful suggestions of his ambitious and ruthless wife, who could never feel at rest while there lived in all her husband's realm one man great enough to be his possible rival. It was by her advice that the king had attached Kenneth Macduff to his court, apparently as an honoured guest, but really as a valuable hostage; and through her eyes the troubled man saw in the elder Macduff's frank loyalty, and in Baccogh's cousinly affection, grounds of suspicion and jealousy that existed nowhere but in his own disturbed conscience and haunted mind.

By slow degrees the change in him reacted on them likewise, and the gulf between the former friends widened daily and hourly, till even the ever-gay and thoughtless Kenneth could not fail to notice it and grieve at it.

It was this thought that clouded the young man's bright face and marred his enjoyment of his favourite sport as he stood at his post in the Tay woods, spear in hand, on the morning of one of the great hunting-parties that Macbeth was constantly giving.

All at once came a rustle in the thicket behind him, a sharp crackle of broken twigs, and round whirled Kenneth with levelled spear, expecting to see his long-watched-for game come bursting forth at last. But in place of wild bull, stag, or wolf, out stepped three stalwart men, all well armed, who came right up to him. Two of them he knew at once as Macbeth's own clansmen, and among his trustiest attendants; the third was a big yellow-bearded Dane.

"Chief Kenneth," said the foremost man, looking every way but at the lad himself, "the king bids us go back with thee to Chaistel-an-Lonach [Castle of the Yews]. There will be no hunt to-day."

(The trusty gillie spoke as he was bidden; but he was wrong, none the less. There *was* to be a hunt that day, the memory of which was to endure for ever.)

"Why so? What hath chanced? Hath aught gone amiss with the king?" asked young Macduff anxiously.

"Ask no questions," said the second man, with sombre emphasis, "for we can tell thee naught."

The tall Dane said nothing, but followed close behind him, while the other two walked at his right hand and his left.

Wondering much, but free as yet from any special anxiety, Kenneth went with his three conductors, too busy with his own thoughts to address them, while they on their part never spoke a word.

But suddenly came a rush and a clatter of hoofs, and a single rider, who seemed to issue from the wood, flew by them like a whirlwind, and went dashing down the narrow breakneck path that led to the Tay.

Kenneth was somewhat surprised at this apparition; for the Scots, as a rule, hunted as well as fought on foot, having little use for horses among their rocky hills and pathless forests. But he was more surprised yet, when, as the horseman flashed past him, he saw, or thought he saw, that this wild rider was no other than his own father!

"Was not that my father, Dougal?" said he hastily to the man on his left.

But none of the three gave him any answer.

The young noble was more and more puzzled, and he now began to feel somewhat uneasy as well. It was quite a new thing for the king to put an end to one of his own hunts ere it had well begun; and when a man of his father's rank and importance was seen galloping off in such desperate haste, without even one of his many attendants, something very serious must have occurred.

Could Macbeth have been struck down by the horn of a stag, which the belief of that age held to be certain death? But no! that could not be, for the hunt had not begun yet. Had some sudden and mortal sickness attacked him, and was Macduff's headlong ride in quest of priest or physician? But that could not be, for his guides had said positively that they acted by the king's own orders.

Then came a thought that made the bold lad's heart leap. Had the Danes made a new descent on the Scottish coast, and was his father riding in such haste to call out the warriors of Fife to meet them? But if this were so, why should he himself, King Macbeth's special friend and companion, be thus sent away from the king's side at the approach of danger? And why should these men who were with him—three of the best fighters in the royal bodyguard—have been withdrawn from their post just when they were most needed ?

In a word, our hero, ponder as he might, could make nothing of it; and of the terrible truth that was soon to burst upon him he had no suspicion whatever.

But it was well for him, or he would have been more troubled still, that Kenneth did not see what followed; for hardly were he and his guards out of sight behind the straggling skirts of the wood, when there was a thunder of charging hoofs, a hoarse clamour of many voices, and a troop of horsemen, fully armed, came bursting out of the forest at furious speed in hot pursuit of the flying Macduff.

" Which way did he go ? " cried one. " There is no man in sight to tell us."

" Southward, I trow ! " called out another. " That way lies his own domain of Fife."

" And lo ! here be fresh hoof-prints," shouted a third, " down the path that leads to the Tay ! "

" After him then, whip and spur ! " roared a terrible voice from the midst of the band, which was that of Macbeth himself. " We will have him yet, if we follow him to the end of the earth ! "

And the whole troop went dashing at full speed,

at the risk of their lives—for their grim king, in
such a mood, was not to be trifled with—down the
steep and broken descent, at the foot of which,
glittering amid its dark thickets, ran the winding
stream of the Tay.

What was the actual cause of this final quarrel
between Macbeth and Macduff no one seemed to
know, nor has it ever been known. But betwixt
two such fierce and untamed spirits, already stirred
up against each other, it needed but a spark to
kindle such a flame as nothing but blood could
quench; and Macduff himself, as he flew helter-
skelter down the hillside, splashing through mud
pools, leaping fallen trees, sending the crashing
stones flying like hail from beneath his horse-hoofs,
had no doubt what would be his fate if overtaken.

"Heaven grant that the ferry-boat be on this
side of the river!" muttered he, as he came crashing through bush and brier out on to the bank of
the Tay; "for if not, I am a dead man!"

But, luckily for him—or this man-hunt would
have ended ere it had well begun—the two ferrymen, knowing that the king and his train were
out hunting that day, and thinking it likely that
some of the hunters might wish to cross the river,

had brought their boat to the northern bank, where it was now lying.

"Hurry, lads; I am on the king's business!" shouted Macduff to the two men as he dashed up to them and sprang from his steaming horse, shooting a hasty glance over his shoulder as he did so, in the fear of seeing his foremost pursuers come dashing over the crest of the ridge above him.

It was the first and last lie that the great Thane of Fife ever told; but, in one terrible sense at least, it was partly true. He *was* on the king's business in that death ride, for on its issue hung King Macbeth's life and his own.

Both men were on their feet in a moment; and Macduff added hurriedly, as he dragged rather than led his panting horse aboard the huge, heavy, punt-like barge that served as a ferry-boat,—

"Neither purse nor scrip bear I with me, in such haste did I set off; and I have naught to pay my passage withal, save this loaf of bread which I snatched from the king's table as I gat me to horse. If that may suffice ye, take it, for I have naught else."

"It needs not that, noble thane," heartily answered one of the two men, who was from Macduff's own county of Fife, and knew him well by sight.

The dark cluster of pursuing riders was still full in view.

"Right glad are we to pleasure thee, pay or no pay. Keep thy loaf for the journey, and God speed thee on thy way!"

And in a trice the two sturdy fellows were propelling the heavy boat across the river, with all the might of their brawny arms.

But quick as they had been, they were not a moment too soon.

The boat had not yet reached the farther bank when over the brow of the ridge above it came dashing a solitary horseman, the foremost of the pursuing riders; and that horseman was no other than Macbeth himself!

The grim king growled a fearful curse under his breath, as he saw that his prey had escaped him once more, just as it seemed fairly in his grasp; but enraged almost to madness as he was, he let no sign of it appear beyond that stifled exclamation, for, with the ruthless foresight and fell concentration of purpose to which Shakespeare has done full justice, he had already grasped the whole situation.

The hunted thane was safe over the river, there was no help for that; and it would be worse than useless to alarm by shouts or threats the two ferrymen, who were already bringing their boat along-

side of the other shore. That Macduff had not
told them the real state of the case could be seen
by their faces, which, plainly visible to Macbeth
where he stood, showed no sign of unusual excitement; and should he himself betray to them, by
an imprudent outburst of rage, how matters really
stood, these men, one of whom was a Fifeman like
Macduff himself, would probably keep the boat on
the other side, and thus make further pursuit impossible.

The only thing to do, in short, was to cross the
river as soon as he could, and run down his chief
foe, without pausing to waste his vengeance on
meaner heads like these.

But the transport of a whole troop of mounted
men, horses and all, was a far longer process than
the mere ferrying over of a single rider; and by
the time they were all across, Macduff had gained
such a start as might give him a fair chance of
escape after all.

But Macbeth was not to be balked of his fell
purpose; and now began the last and most terribly
exciting stage of this deadly race, which, little as
the wild racers could then foresee it, was to be
famous long after they were all dead and gone.
Ages later harper and minstrel were still singing

in rude ballad verse how King Macbeth hunted Thane Macduff from the Tay to the Forth, for life and death :——

> " They have ridden o'er hill, they have ridden o'er dale,
>   They have ridden o'er moorland gray ;
> The race that they ran in the early morn
>   Was running at close of day.

> " Thro' tangled thicket and rushing flood
>   The good steeds panted amain ;
> They ran not for prize of silver or gold,
>   But the life of our wightest [hardiest] thane."

On, on, across the shallow pebbly bed of the Earn, through the wooded passes of the Ochil Hills, past the wide, smooth, shining expanse of Loch Leven and the shadowy ridge of Bennarty. Hurrah! he is on the soil of his native Fife at last; and yonder, far to the south, the broad sweep of the noble Forth, the river on which his own castle stands, glitters in the westering sun amid the green slopes of its guardian hills.

But though the bold man had escaped thus far, he was by no means safe yet.

Every time he looked back the dark cluster of pursuing riders was still full in view, and even seemed to be gradually creeping nearer and nearer; and now he saw all at once, with secret dismay, that his gallant courser, which had hitherto borne him on like the wind, was beginning to flag.

The hunted man set his teeth grimly, and bending forward in the saddle, sped on toward the south.

But all at once he started slightly, and his whole face seemed to harden like frozen clay; for right in front of him yawned a wide, deep rocky chasm, completely barring his way!

To try such a leap with a tired horse was all but certain death; but death was even more certain if he did not, for he knew what mercy he had to expect if taken. Patting the brave beast's neck caressingly, he called it cheerily by name, and dashed at the yawning gulf before him.

It was a terrible leap, and even the daring Macduff held his breath as he felt himself shoot out over the brink.

There was a sudden shock, a deafening crash, and a huge mass of earth and stones broke away from beneath the charger's hind hoofs and fell thundering into the gulf below. But the thane was safe over, and answering with a laugh of cheery defiance the yell of fury that burst from his baffled pursuers, on he went once more.

To follow him over such a leap with spent

horses was more than any of the chasers, even
Macbeth himself, cared to do. Nor, in truth, was
it needful; for the king's keen eye quickly espied
a point where, barely two hundred paces to the
right, the chasm narrowed enough to be easily
cleared.

But in the meantime Macduff had once more got
a fair start, and in this match against time with
death every yard was of importance.

Ha! what was that tall dark shadow which the
hunted man suddenly saw far ahead of him? Was
it only a jutting crag? or was it—could it be—
the tower of his own castle by the Forth?

It was, it was! and his gallant horse seemed to
know it too, and rallying the last remnant of its
failing strength, flew onward like an arrow.

And now the excitement of this life-and-death
race mounted to a height. Nearer and nearer came
the friendly castle; but nearer and nearer, too, came
the pursuing foes. Could his horse hold out? It
seemed more than doubtful, for it was plainly failing fast; and every time he looked up at the distant tower, it appeared farther off than before.

To all appearance the hard-pressed man had now
but one chance left. The sun was fast sinking,
and as he glanced back to measure the distance

that still lay between him and his pursuers, it struck him that if he could not reach the castle ere they caught him up, he might escape by throwing himself from his horse, and creeping away through the thickets in the darkness. He knew this whole region by heart, and—

Crash! Macduff felt himself shot through the air like a stone from a sling. His spent horse had put its foot in a hole, and come down on its head, hurling him from the saddle in its fall.

Happily the thick bushes among which he alighted saved him from any worse hurt than a few bruises; but he saw at a glance that his trusty steed was lamed outright, and his foes were coming up at full speed!

For one moment even the bold thane gave himself up for lost; and then a sudden thought flashed upon him which might save him yet. Snatching off his plaid, he flung it into a deep, bushy hollow on the left; and then, slipping away behind the thick undergrowth, he ran like a hunted deer toward his castle, which now stood full in view on its rocky height, barely a mile away.

But all his speed would not have saved him had not his pursuers, on coming to the spot, been misled by the sight of the fallen horse and the plaid among the bushes below into the belief that Macduff had been thrown and killed, and that it was his body which they saw lying in the hollow.

The few moments that it took to undeceive them saved the hunted thane once more ; but as he broke from the thickets into the open ground beyond, his foes caught sight of him again, and dashed after him with a yell like a pack of hungry wolves !

Driven to desperation, Macduff, with what little breath he had left, blew on his bugle as he ran the blast that was his signal to open the castle gate on his return from hunting ; and an instant noise and bustle within told that the warning had been heard.

And now he was at the foot of the castle hill itself, and now he saw the heavy gate above him swing open, but the pursuing shout and hoof tramp came closer and closer at his heels. Gasping, quivering, stumbling at every step, he dashed blindly up the steep rocky slope. A wild clamour of mingled outcries—a clatter of horse-hoofs close in the rear— a hovering mist before his eyes—the leading horsemen were already within a few paces of him—

One mighty bound carried the hunted man right into the sheltering archway—the ponderous gate clanged to behind him—and he was safe at last !

CHAPTER X.

IN THE FOREST AT MIDNIGHT.

WHILE the elder Macduff was thus flying for his life, his son, many miles away, was face to face with an almost equal peril of another kind.

The Castle of the Yews, to which his three guards had been ordered to escort him, was originally but a small timber hunting-lodge, built by King Malcolm II., Macbeth's grandfather, for his own convenience when "driving the deer" in the Tay forests. But Macbeth himself, as keen a sportsman as even his great contemporary William the Conqueror, had so altered and enlarged it that it was now quite a strong place, judged by the standard of that time.

Lying in the heart of a thick forest, and shut in on every side with gloomy masses of yew trees, which came up to within a few hundred yards of the gate itself, the Chaistel-an-Lonach was a sombre-looking place at best; and Kenneth Macduff, though he had

often been there before, and was well used to its
dismal aspect, felt himself shudder as he entered
it, without knowing why, as if some dim foreboding
of the horror to come had suddenly darkened his
bright and buoyant spirit.

But all at once a cheering thought came to brighten
him up again.

If the Danes were really raiding their coasts anew,
Macbeth must be expecting some of the invaders to
attack his castle, while the rest met him in the field ;
and in that case, it was only natural that Kenneth
and these three picked men—and, no doubt, many
others as well—should be sent to strengthen the
garrison against the coming assault.

That must be it ; and though the brave lad would
have much preferred to fight by the king's side in
the open field, even this was better than being kept
idle while the spoiler's foot was on Scottish soil.

His three mute conductors, still as silent as ever,
led him up a steep, narrow stair to a room which,
though small, was tolerably comfortable for that age ;
but its sole furniture consisted of a rude table and
a heavy wooden "settle," or bench, and in the corner
a rough straw pallet, which any stable-boy of our age
would disdain, though a Scottish noble of the eleventh
century thought it quite good enough for *him*.

The table was quickly spread with food, to which young Macduff, already as hungry as a hawk, at once devoted himself so eagerly that he did not see the pitying look cast at him by the tall Dane—who seemed the least savage of these grim warders—as he went slowly out of the room.

The other two, after lingering for a moment as if to make sure that the guest had all he required, slouched away in turn with an air of well-assumed carelessness; but hardly had the door closed behind the last man when our hero was startled to hear a heavy wooden bar shot across it from the outside, thus making him a prisoner.

This, then, was the true meaning of all these strange proceedings: he had been brought here, not as a guest or a soldier, but as a captive!

In his first flush of anger at finding himself thus ensnared, and even disarmed—for the spear that he had placed against the wall was gone—the bold lad sprang up as fiercely as a trapped tiger. But a moment's thought told him, for he was as shrewd as daring, that nothing was to be gained by violence.

The iron bars which crossed the opening that served as a window forbade any passage there; and though his strength, with the heavy bench for a battering-ram, might shatter the door, he could not do so without making noise enough to alarm the whole castle, and perhaps cause his removal to a far less tolerable dungeon.

But why was he made prisoner at all? His guards had said that they acted by the king's orders. But how could *he* have given Macbeth any cause to treat him as a criminal?

On this point, however, he was not left long in doubt. As he went once more to the window, in the faint hope—which was soon swept away—that the bars might possibly be dislodged, he heard a gruff voice say in the courtyard below,—

"Comes the king back soon, brother Fergus?"

"I trow not," replied a second voice; "for if, as one said but now, he is off with his train in chase of Thane Macduff, methinks that hunt will not be over very soon."

"Thou art right, comrade," chimed in a third man; "such a rider, on such a horse, will show goodly sport ere he be caught. But whether he be caught or no, we have his son here, hard and fast; and with such a surety in hand the king holdeth Thane Macduff tied by the foot, let him flutter as he will."

Every drop of blood in the startled lad's veins tingled as he listened. This, then, was the meaning of his father's headlong flight; and should he escape, his own son was to serve the king as a hostage for him!

It was characteristic of the frank and chivalrous generosity of Kenneth Macduff's nature that his first feeling was a pang of bitter regret that Macbeth, the man whom he had so loved and trusted, could be capable of a deed like this. But that regret was instantly swallowed up in a passion of burning wrath at the thought that he—*he*—was meant to serve as a tool to bend his own father into some act unworthy of him.

Come what might, that should never be. Escape he must, at all hazards; and at that very moment flashed across his mind a scheme by which he might hope to do so. But his plan could not be carried out till dark; and in the meantime he must eat and drink to keep up his strength, for he would need it all.

To the bold lad's feverish impatience it seemed as if the sun would never go down; but it sank at last, and in a trice the room was pitch dark.

Now for it! Hastily setting up the bench on end, he perched the table a-top of it, and then, giving a terrific scream, knocked down bench and table with a crash, as if the whole tower were falling.

Instantly there was a stir and a clamour of voices below, a tramp of hurrying feet up the stair, and the door was unbarred and flung open, and in burst half a dozen men, all but touching in the gloom their unseen prisoner, who had planted himself in a corner close to the door.

The moment the last man was in, Kenneth slipped quietly out and glided down the stair as noiselessly as he could, the slight sound that he made being drowned by the shouting and trampling of the men above as they tumbled over the bench in the dark or bumped against each other.

"Bring a torch, quick!" cried one of them excitedly. "The lad is not on his pallet, nor can I find him anywhere."

But ere the torch could be brought, our hero had gained the courtyard and stolen across it undetected. He knew that the outer gate was shut and guarded and the encircling palisade too high to be scaled without a ladder; but he had marked from his window a tall tree on one side of the court, thrusting out a huge limb so far that by clutching the end of it he could swing himself up on to the top of the stockade.

In a trice he had done it, and leaping down outside, flew like an arrow over the open ground to the sheltering wood beyond. He reached it not a whit too soon, for just then the rising moon broke forth above the black tree-tops in all its glory ; and Kenneth, guessing by the growing din from the castle that his jailers had discovered the trick played on them, and their important captive's escape, made haste to bury himself in the depths of the forest.

But all at once he was startled by a sound of voices close to him, and he had barely time to crawl under a clump of bushes when three men stole by, in whom, as they crossed the moonlight, he knew his silent guards of the morning.

At first he thought they were in pursuit of *him*, but he suddenly heard one of them mutter as they went by,—

" Can they be come already ?   Methought I heard but now something stir in the thicket hard by."

" It was but the wind rustling in the boughs," said one of the comrades.   " But hark ! what sound was that in front of us ? "

" Be ready ! they come ! " whispered the third man hoarsely.

Sure enough, at that very instant a sound of steps and voices and of crackling boughs was plainly heard a little way ahead.

All that followed was the work of a moment.   A rush of the three ruffians to the spot, a noise of trampling, blows, and scuffling; a deep groan, and then a voice shouting, or rather screaming,—

" Fly, Fillan !   Fly for thy life ! "

The words came forth shrill and strained, like a cry of mortal agony, and the voice which spoke was that of Macbeth's cousin, Thane Baccogh of Lochaber !

CHAPTER XI.

FLYING FOR LIFE.

IN spite of his dying father's warning, Fillan would have had no chance of escape, for one of the cutthroats was close at his heels, had not young Macduff, who took in the whole situation at a glance, flown to the rescue, unarmed as he was. Employing once more the device that had served him so well already, Kenneth set up a terrific yell, and, ere the murderer could strike, leaped right on his back.

Scared out of his wits, the ruffian, thinking himself in the claws of the wood-demons with whom the belief of that age peopled every forest in Europe, made the air ring with a howl of terror, and shaking off his assailant with a convulsive effort, dashed blindly away through bush and briar, still yelling as he went, while his two fellow-murderers, naturally superstitious, and disturbed by the bloody work which they had just done, rushed headlong after him, echoing his cries as they ran.

Meanwhile Kenneth had raised his friend Fillan, who had been flung to the ground, and was much relieved to find him unhurt; but ere he could say a word the Lochaber lad called out,—

"My father—come quick! He may yet live."

They flew to the spot; but the fell work had been done only too well, and the gallant thane was already beyond all human aid.

Even with the risk of the assassins returning at any moment to kill them both, these brave lads could not bear to leave that beloved form unburied, to be torn by wolf and raven; and, having no means of digging a grave, they laid the body reverently in a deep, narrow cleft, and covered it with stones and dead boughs.

Then Fillan sought and found his dropped hunting-spear, his comrade armed himself with the dead warrior's dirk and a spear let fall by one of the scared cutthroats in his flight; and that done, the two friends, knowing well that there was no safety for them so near the fatal castle, hastened to bury themselves in the depths of the wood.

As they went Fillan heard the tale of young Macduff's adventures; and then Kenneth, who was burning to know the meaning of this mysterious attack on two such universal favourites as Thane

Baccogh and his son, questioned his comrade in turn, and listened with mingled horror and disgust to what the other had to tell.

That the king and his train *had* gone in chase of Thane Macduff the speaker had seen with his own eyes, though he knew nothing of the cause of this sudden enmity.   The hunting - party being thus broken up, he and his father had lingered about for a time, hoping for some sport on their own account; and then, finding no game, and seeing no chance of Macbeth's speedy return, they decided to go back to the Castle of the Yews and await him there.

Back they went, and were all but in sight of the place when the lurking ruffians made that attack which Kenneth had come just in time to witness.

" And I heard yon felon who would have slain me," ended Fillan, with grim emphasis, " cry to his fellow- rogues, ' The king bade us kill both ! ' What cause of displeasure my father or I can have given him, I wot not ; but this murder was the deed of Macbeth, and of no other man under heaven."

Kenneth was speechless with indignation and horror ; but gladly as he would have doubted the hideous tale, it was only too fully and terribly confirmed by what he had himself heard and seen.

The words and behaviour of the murderers had

proved beyond a doubt that they were on the watch
for their victims, and had come thither on purpose
to meet them ; and two of the three were Macbeth's
own clansmen, and among the most trusted soldiers
of his bodyguard. It was now but too plain that
this was no chance affray, no attack for the purpose
of robbery, but a deliberate and well-laid ambush ;
and the man who could thus plot the cold-blooded
murder of his nearest kinsmen and friends was at
that very moment hunting to the death Kenneth
Macduff's own father !

The tale ended, the two fugitives went along side
by side for a long time without a word, each buried
in his own gloomy thoughts. But at last Fillan came
to a sudden halt and asked his comrade, with the air
of one to whom the idea had only just occurred, where
they were going.

Strangely enough, this question, though it might
well have seemed the first thing to be thought of,
had never till then occurred to either of the two,
whose sole idea at the outset had been to put as
great a distance as possible between themselves and
the pursuit which they expected and dreaded.

But now that the query was put to him so directly,
young Macduff answered it as promptly as if he had
been thinking of nothing else.

"Where should we go, but to my father's castle
on the Forth? If he hath escaped these wolves that
are on his track, there will he be found; and if not,
so much the more reason that *I* should be there to
put myself at the head of our vassals, and defend
my mother and sisters from yon murdering caitiff
who hath slain thy father, and perchance mine
too."

"Well said!" cried Fillan heartily; "and if aught
that I can do may help them or thee, be assured thou
wilt not find me backward. Let us on, then, with
what speed we may."

Strong, active, and well used to long, forced
marches, the two wanderers went onward at a pace
which, considering the scanty light and the broken
ground, was really marvellous. Only at long intervals
did they halt to take breath, and to make quite sure
that they were still heading in the right direction;
and when day dawned they were so far from the
castle as to be safe from any risk of being overtaken.

"Now, comrade," said Kenneth, halting and sitting
down, "let us eat ere we go farther. When they
brought me food yester-eve, I bestowed in my pouch
all I could not eat, knowing that I might need it,
so I trow we need fear no famine yet awhile."

"Nor need we fear it even when our store is

spent," cried his friend cheerily, "so long as these woods hold game and our hands hold spears."

At sunrise they swam the Tay, which was luckily pretty low at that point. All that day they went southward at their best speed, and as the sun began to sink they found themselves fairly on the soil of Fife at last, for in those days its boundaries were far wider than they are now.

Seeing that the lowering sky boded a coming storm, Fillan proposed to ask a night's lodging— always freely given in that age of rough hospitality —at a small farmhouse that had just come in sight a little way ahead, but young Macduff, more wary and less impulsive, was still hesitating, when two horsemen were seen coming up from the south, horses and riders standing clearly out in the red glow of sunset.

"These be Macbeth's men, by their garb," said Kenneth, who had inherited his father's keen eye, as he whisked his comrade behind a sheltering bush— "I take them to be some of the band that chased my father yester-eve returning from their chase."

"Then must we get us hence with all speed," quoth his friend, "for belike they mean to halt here."

"No doubt they do," said the other coolly, "but

for that very reason must we *not* get us hence; for
I would fain hear all they have to tell, and methinks
they will gossip awhile with their host ere they ride
on.   Hither, to the right, and follow me close."

Creeping from clump to clump of the straggling
bushes on their right, the two bold lads succeeded in
getting round to the other side of the house unseen
by any one.

Once there, Kenneth pointed out to his friend, with
a meaning nod, a huge stack of dried bracken and
dead boughs reared up against the house wall as a
store of fuel.   The deep, narrow channel of a tiny
brook, all but dry at that season, enabled them to
crawl up to this fuel pile unseen; and in a trice
they had crept beneath it, tugging forward an
armful or two of bracken so as to be completely
hidden.

They reached this lurking-place none too soon, for
hardly were they hid when they heard the hoof-
tramp sweep right up to the house, and then a deep,
hoarse voice called out,—

" Methinks, friend Eachin, it were well to breathe
our steeds awhile, for they seem wellnigh spent;
and if there be any food to be had here, I wot
well I can find an appetite.   What-ho, goodman
within there ! "

Out came the goodman of the house, a short, sturdy fellow, whose broad, heavy, light-complexioned face, thick yellow hair, and peculiar dress showed him to be a "Flanderkin," one of those Flemish colonists already numerous south of the Forth, and found here and there even in Scotland proper.

"Good-even to thee, neighbour," said the man who had spoken, as he and his comrade leaped from their jaded horses. "Hast thou perchance an oaten bannock [oatcake] by thee, and a sup of milk to wash it down withal?"

"Both shalt thou have, and welcome," cried the Fleming heartily; "and if ye walk by my rede [counsel] ye will bide here with me this night, for yon sky bodes a storm—ay, and a heavy one."

"I thank thee for thy goodwill, friend," said the other, "but we ride at the king's hest [order], and *he* brooks no loitering."

"No, truly," chimed in Eachin; "such a race as we rode yester-morn my horse never ran before —hey, Moraig?"

"I trow not," said the first man, "nor ever shall again, methinks, unless a witch were on his back."

"Ye have gone a-hunting with King Macbeth, then, belike?" said the Fleming.

"Ay, truly," said Moraig, with a grin; "hunting

a goodly stag that runneth right swiftly, whose tines [horns] deal ugly blows. Men call him Thane Macduff."

"Thane Macduff, say'st thou?" echoed the farmer, in amazement. "What hath *he* done, then, to be thus hunted?"

"I know not, nor care," said the clansman bluntly. "Whom Macbeth bids me chase, I chase; whom Macbeth bids me slay, I slay. Howbeit, though I chased Macduff, I slew him not, for he escaped us after all."

The listening Kenneth drew a long, deep breath of intense relief.

"Gladly would I hear how that befell," said the Fleming, with visible interest; "and if ye have no leisure to come indoors, I will bring some food out to you, and ye can tell the tale as ye break your fast."

The food soon appeared, and between his mouthfuls Moraig told in a few forcible words, little dreaming *who* were listening, the story of the man-hunt and of Macduff's final plunge through his castle gate, just as they thought him at their mercy.

"And then," struck in Eachin, "we beat upon the gate and clamoured for entrance; but for a space none gave us any heed. At last one with a gray beard looked over the wall to us, and asked roughly what rabble we were who dared thus to knock so rudely at the Thane of Fife's gate, and bade us be gone straightway, or they would let fly at us from the walls with arrows."

Here a huge draught of milk stopped the speaker for a moment, and Moraig made use of the pause to chime in once more,—

"But then came forward Macbeth himself, whose horse had fallen with him in mounting the hill and hurt him somewhat, else had he done it before, and bade them open to *the king;* and I warrant ye that word made the knaves change their note, the more when they saw that it was in truth he himself. So they opened the gates to us—howbeit they took a weary long time to do it—and in we all went, horse and man.

"Then Macbeth bade them summon Thane Macduff, saying that he must speak with him straightway, and they told him that the Thane was gone to his lady's bower, and there would he be found. Thither went the king in haste; but the bower door was made fast within."

"And then," said Eachin, taking up again his part in the duet, "Macbeth smote on the door, and bade open and give the king entrance. But none

replied, though there came from within as it were
a sound of moving to and fro.   Then the king,
deeming they did but mock him, waxed wroth, and
bade break the door ; which when we had done, we
found no soul within."

Here the speaker made an impressive pause.

" The saints be good to us ! " muttered the startled
Fleming, making the sign of the cross with a
trembling hand.   " And what befell next ? "

" Then," went on Eachin, " we all, even the king
himself, stood amazed, and wist not what to do ; and
the same old gray-beard who had threatened us
from the wall spake under his breath, with his teeth
chattering as though it were midwinter,—

" ' I have ever heard that our lady, Dame Granua,
hath power to vanish away when she will, and be
found in some other place ; and now I see full well
'tis true.' "

" What say'st thou to that, comrade ? " whispered
Fillan to his new friend, with a superstitious shudder.
" Hath thy mother, in very deed, skill in magic ? "

" Think'st thou, then," retorted Kenneth with un-
disguised indignation, though in the same cautious
tone, " that *my* mother, a Christian lady, could have
aught to do with unlawful arts ?   There is a secret
passage beneath the earth, leading forth of our castle,

which is known to none save my father only, and
by it, no doubt, have they all escaped the clutches
of yon murderer, God be praised for it!'"

Just then Moraig, in his turn, took up the thread
of the tale once more.

"At that moment," said he, "came a shout from
above, and one of our band, who had gone up to
the walls to see what he could spy, called to us
that there was a light bark lying close inshore, and
that three womenfolk and an armed man had just
got on board of her.

"Then 'Haste, haste!' was the word; but haste
as we might, we were too late. Ere we could reach
the bank, away flew the bark down the river like
a seabird, and from her came a voice that was like
the voice of Thane Macduff: 'Farewell, Macbeth!
thou shalt see me again in an ill hour for thee!'*
Not a word said the king to that, but he looked
full grim, and I heard him mutter through his
clenched teeth, 'No matter! if the father hath
'scaped me, I still hold fast the son.'"

Fillan, as he lay, felt the bracken around him
quiver with the silent but hearty laugh that was

---

* Such is probably the true account of this famous incident; for
Macbeth's alleged massacre of Macduff's family, of which Shakespeare has made such terrible use, rests on a more than doubtful
tradition.

shaking the whole frame of his comrade, who, guessing at once that these men bore Macbeth's order to keep Kenneth a close prisoner, was enjoying the thought of the surprise that awaited them when they should find the bird flown.

A few minutes later the two messengers rode off again, and hardly were they out of sight when the storm burst in all its fury. A flash — a roll of thunder; and then came the fierce hiss and patter of the torrent rain, through which the furious wind howled and shrieked like a troubled spirit.

But not a drop could penetrate the thick canopy of bracken and boughs that shielded the two lads, who, warmly wrapped in their plaids, fell quietly asleep, not to wake till day was breaking.

Bright and clear it dawned after the night's storm, and our heroes, scrambling out, lost no time in slipping away into the shelter of the nearest thicket, where, as they shared their last remaining morsels of food, young Macduff said gravely to his comrade,—

"Fillan, lad, it behoves us now to take good counsel what we should do. Since Macbeth's men hold my father's castle, there is no place for us there; and, in good sooth, I know not where to go."

"I do, then," cried Fillan, pleased to help, in his

turn, the friend who had saved his life; "we will
betake ourselves straightway to Gryffyth ap-Llewellyn,
the King of North Wales."

"The King of North Wales!" echoed Kenneth,
staring. "Why should we go to *him*? And what
manner of welcome would he give us, who slayeth,
men say, all strangers that fall into his hands?"

"That is but leasing [lying]," said the other.
"He is ever dour [stern] to the Saxons, for they
are his foes; but as for those that come to him in
peace, peace they shall find. And, moreover, I myself am of kin to Gryffyth, after a sort."

"Ha!" cried Kenneth, "I bethink me, now thou
speak'st of it, thou didst tell me once of an uncle
of thine who is King Gryffyth's friend and kinsman."

"Even so," said Fillan. "When my Uncle Murdoch was outlawed he fled to Wales, where he did
Gryffyth good service in his wars with the Saxons
of Mercia, and wedded a princess of Powys-Land
who was of the king's blood. Now, it befell that
in these wars Uncle Murdoch took captive a cunning
man of the Saxons, skilled in leech-craft [doctoring],
and right deft withal at pricking out the strange
figures wherewith Saxon warriors are wont to adorn
their bodies. Thou hast heard of them, belike?"

Young Macduff nodded, for the curious fondness

of the Saxons for tattooing their skins with all kinds
of strange figures was well known everywhere.

"Then my uncle caused mark on his breast, by
this cunning man, the figure that Gryffyth the king
bore on his banner—the Lion of Wales (for Gryffyth
is aye called the Lion King) slaying the White
Horse of the Saxons. Thereat was the king well
pleased, and vowed that he who bore that mark
should ever be welcome to him ; for which cause my
uncle, when he came to visit us eight years agone,
after his outlawry was taken off, marked on my breast
—having learned the art from this Saxon captive—
the same figure that was on his own. Behold !"

He threw back his head as he spoke, and there,
sure enough, was the figure described, plainly tattooed
on his chest, just beneath the throat.

"Good !" cried Kenneth cheerily. "No other letter
of credence do we need, I trow; and, happily, it is so
writ that it cannot well be lost. To Wales let us go,
then, and may God be with us on our way !"

Thus did our heroes set off on a tramp of more than
two hundred miles through a half-savage country,
without money or supplies of any kind, and with a
very fair chance of being murdered on the way. But
in that age such trifles were little thought of, and these
daring lads held them as lightly as any man alive.

CHAPTER XII.

BESET BY THE "WHITE MANTLES."

BLACK and thick against the clear frosty sky rose the smoke of ruined hamlet and blazing town all along the Welsh border, on a fine winter morning in the fatal January of 1046.

Far as the eye could reach, the whole land was one black and blasted desert, for this unhappy region was never at peace. Saxon slew and plundered Welshman, Welshman slew and plundered Saxon; and when this ceaseless riot of blood and ruin slackened at one point, it was only to break out with fresh fury at another.

Amid the smouldering ashes of their homes dead men—ay, and dead women and children too—lay rotting unburied on every side, to be torn by the carrion birds which nested in the half-burned ruins, and by the wolves that prowled unchecked through farmyard and orchard. Those who have seen how sad and terrible a thing war can be even in this humane age of ours, can judge what it must have been in days when mercy was unknown, and when the passage of an army meant ruin to every home and death to every living creature.

Not easily, in truth, could the gloomiest fancy surpass the multiplied horrors contained in that one brief, simple phrase of the quaint old Saxon chronicles :—

"Nowe in those daies were hotte warres on the Marches of Wales."

Such was the scene on which two dusty, weather-tanned figures, who seemed to have travelled long and far, looked down from the brow of a low ridge among the border hills of North Wales, in the growing splendour of a bright winter sunrise.

"Well, if this be the handiwork of thy kinsman King Gryffyth," said the taller of the two, with a grim smile, "methinks, friend Fillan, in seeking refuge with *him* we have but done as did the stag that leaped over a precipice to save itself from the hounds."

"Judge not the king too hastily, comrade Kenneth," said Fillan stoutly. "These Saxons of Mercia are his sworn foes, and he hath but done to them as they have many a time done to him, and would do again were he not too strong for them. But who be these ? Some of Gryffyth's own men, I trow."

As he spoke, a crowd of wild forms came swarming out, in a long straggling line, from the hills that lay to the south, and swept on toward the foot of the ridge on which the two young men were standing.

Wild-looking fellows they were, these newcomers, bare-armed and bare-limbed, with no defence for their feet against the sharp stones but rough goatskin sandals, and clad simply in the plain white frock or cloak (a survival of the "tunic" of their Roman conquerors) whence they took their name of "the white mantles of Wales"—those dreaded warriors whose boast it was that they presented their bare limbs and light mantles to the swords and spears of their foes as boldly as if sheathed in armour of proof.

Most of these strange soldiers were bareheaded as well, hardly one-half having caps of steel or hardened skin ; but their long thick hair, tossing loose on their shoulders like a mane, was an ample substitute. By far the greater number marched on foot, though some of the foremost were mounted on those small shaggy untiring horses, very like the Shetland ponies of our own time, for which Wales was then so famous.

Nor were their arms less barbaric than their

aspect: small bows and heavy iron-headed arrows, light goatskin shields, barbed spears, short broad-bladed swords (another legacy of the Roman conquest), and strong steel-headed javelins, in the use of which the Welsh of that age were fatally skilled.

To the two lookers-on the idea of calling this armed mob an "army" was less strange than it would have been to a Norman or Saxon soldier of that day, for both were well used to see, in their own armies in Scotland, plenty of men with hardly clothes enough to cover them, and armed with clubs, hatchets, bill-hooks, wood knives, or sharp stakes hardened in the fire.

They were still gazing down at the wild procession with simple, boyish interest, when a sudden bustle among the Welsh warriors, a general pointing of hands upward, and then a shrill, ear-piercing shout, or rather yell, told that they had been seen.

"They have caught sight of us," said Fillan, as coolly as ever; "and now is the time to see if the spell of this mark on my breast will work or no. Stand fast, comrade Kenneth, and let us meet these bawlers as Scottish men should do."

So saying, he folded his arms on his chest and awaited with perfect composure the advancing savages, more than a score of whom were already darting up the slope right toward them.

But when the fierce men saw their intended victims, so far from attempting to fly, quietly await- ing their coming, they began to pause, partly in honest admiration of the strangers' courage, and partly in superstitious awe at their seemingly un- accountable calmness. Who could they be, these two unknown men, whom an armed host could not dismay ? Surely they must be supernatural beings, against whom no mortal arm had any power !

Such a thing seemed quite possible to the wild mountaineers, who were even more superstitious than the average men of their day, and within a few paces of those two immovable forms the boldest of the onrushing Welsh came to a doubtful halt.

Then Fillan, standing motionless, spoke for the first time,—

" Faree Gryffydd ap - Llewellyn ? " (Where is Gryffyth, son of Llewellyn ?)

The hesitating Welsh looked visibly relieved, as if suddenly convinced that they had to do with mortal men after all ; but at the same time they seemed more amazed than ever, both at being greeted in their own tongue by one who was clearly no Cymrian, and at hearing these solitary and defenceless strangers ask so boldly for their terrible king.

"And who are ye who would see the Lion King of the Cymry face to face?" asked a tall man with long gray moustaches, who seemed a kind of officer among these wild men of war.

Fillan's only reply was to extend his right hand toward the banner that floated over the Welshmen below, which bore the rude effigy of a lion dragging down a white horse, while with the other hand he threw open his rough jacket and pointed to the same figure on his own breast.

Then, as the startled Welsh gazed at it with eyes that seemed bursting from their sockets, the young Scot called out in their own tongue, loud enough to be heard by all,—

"Gryffydd y ladd Mor-gan!" (Gryffyth slays the man from the sea), a name given by the Welsh to their Saxon and Anglo-Danish neighbours, as having come from beyond the seas.

The deep impression already made on the Cymrian warriors by the sight of their king's badge on this stranger's breast was deepened tenfold by these words, for they formed the title of a famous war-song composed by a renowned Welsh bard of that day, and had long been the war-cry of all King Gryffyth's men.

The magic words were answered with a joyous shout by all who heard them, and in a moment Fillan was caught up and borne in triumph down the hill in the arms of the very men who had just been about to take his life, while others carried young Macduff in the same way.

A few words of explanation from the old chief to the expectant crowd below called forth a fresh shout that woke every echo of the hills around, and at once the wild mountain men came flocking about our heroes, grasping their hands cordially, pressing food and drink on them, and bidding them heartily welcome to the land of the Cymry.

Slight as was Fillan's knowledge of Welsh, it was so far like his own Celtic speech as to let him gather without much trouble, from the talk of those around him, that they were, as he had already guessed, returning from a successful raid into the border lands of the great Saxon earldom of Mercia, which then included all the midland counties of England.

It was, in fact, the vanguard of Gryffyth's own army that they had met, on its march to a place a few miles away called "Curig Cogh" (Red Cliff), where the king had a country palace. Gryffyth himself was expected there on the following day with the main army, and it would then be decided whether to go home with their booty or turn back for one final blow at the Saxon levies hastily called out to repel them.

As may be supposed, the first thing Fillan did was to tell his new friends who he was, and ask for his uncle by the name of "Moradag ap-Dhonuill" (Murdoch, son of Donald). But the gray-haired chief to whom he spoke shook his head sadly, and replied by pointing down with one hand and up with the other —the usual way of announcing a death, as implying that the body had gone down into the grave and the soul up to heaven.

This was a heavy blow to the warm-hearted Scottish lad, who had been looking forward with eagerness, all through his weary journey from the far north, to meeting his long-lost uncle once more. But even in this bitter grief it was some comfort to find that the dead man's name was still remembered and cherished among the wild men with whom his fortunes had been so strangely linked, and that the symbol of brotherhood bequeathed by him to his nephew had lost nothing of its power.

The fact, too, that our heroes were Scots added something, no doubt, to the warmth of their new comrades' welcome, for the northern Celt of Scotland and the southern Celt of Wales were alike sworn foes to the Saxon, who had dealt heavy blows to both; and the practised eyes of the Cymrian chiefs saw at a glance that these two tall, active, stalwart young fellows would be recruits worth having in their ranks when they next crossed steel with the "sons of Hengist."

As it was out of the question for their great king's friend and kinsman to be let march on foot like a common man, the Welsh, before starting again, hoisted Fillan on the back of a shaggy little pony with a hammer-shaped head, and a mane as rough as the hair of King Harold Horrid-locks.

Young Macduff, who shone with the reflected light of his friend's glory, was also provided with a pony, so small that his long gaunt limbs all but touched the ground on either side; and then Father Dawfydd (David), a Welsh monk of Caerleon, "chaplain of the forces" to this destroying host, came up and gave them his blessing—

"May the good Lord be with ye both, and give ye grace and strength to slay many a Saxon!"

And with this characteristic benediction the march was resumed.

CHAPTER XIII.

THE LION KING.

MIRTH and revel were at their height in the hall of Curig Cogh, and the wild banqueters revelled with all the boyish, unthinking gaiety of men well used to pass at any moment from feast to fray, or from fray to feast, and to enjoy both with equal zest.

To the two young Scots as they sat at the Welsh king's board it almost seemed as if they were at home once more, for every detail of the barbaric feasts to which they were used at the court of Scotland, or at their own castles in the far north, was here, point for point. The huge fire blazing in the centre of the floor, the thick black smoke that rolled through the hall, the flaming, crackling torches and soot-blackened rafters, the gray-haired harpers chanting wild ballads of war and havoc, the floor strewn with filthy rushes, and the big hairy wolf-hounds couching on them, the half-savage feasters gnawing the meat from the bones like wild beasts, and shaking off the shower of sparks that fell ceaselessly on their shaggy hair and matted beards—all were there.

The same rude abundance of good cheer, too, that had marked the Scottish feasts was a leading feature of this Welsh banquet. Sheep roasted whole, goats and kids boiled in their own skins, and stags' haunches served up entire were the chief dishes; and the drinking-horns brimmed with strong Welsh "crw" (ale), while for those whose tastes were simpler there was an unstinted supply of milk—always a favourite drink in Wales—and a kind of mead made of honey and water flavoured with the juice of whortle-berries.

But the central figure of that wild revel was so different in every way from what our heroes had expected, that they could not withdraw their eyes from him.

After all the startling tales they had heard of King Gryffyth's almost superhuman daring, his countless feats of desperate valour, his unbroken success in war, and his yet more amazing immunity from death or even severe hurts among the spears and axes on which he was always the first to fling himself, the Scots fully expected the Lion King to be a giant like Asbiorn of Northumbria, or Kenneth's

adopted brother, Harold, Sigurd's son, of Norway—
huge, bulky, irresistibly strong, and towering above
the tallest of his sturdy warriors.

And well might it be so; for in Wales at that
period any advantage of superior height and bulk
(always prized by half-savage races) was so highly
valued that the title of honour given to the princes
and chiefs around Gryffyth's throne was "Uckelwyr,"
literally "tall men." But in place of all this, the
Scots beheld a small, slender, slight-limbed man, with
hands and feet as delicate as a lady's, who was much
less in height than themselves, and looked almost
dwarfish amid the towering forms around him.

Nor was the great king's rank shown by any
richness of dress. His feet and arms were bare; he
wore the plain white tunic that clad all his followers;
and his sole royal insignia were the "eudorchawg,"
or collar of twisted gold wire, round his sun-burned
neck, and the simple gold circlet (shaped like the
ring of black gum worn by a Zulu warrior of our
day) that glittered through the mane of dark-red
hair that flowed down to his shoulders. But neither
crown nor gold chain were needed to enhance the
calm dignity of his commanding look and noble
features, on which nature itself had written, in
characters that all might read, "This is a king."

One other token of royalty, however, the warrior-king of Wales had adopted, and a very strange one it seemed to the two young Scots.

Gryffyth's bare feet rested in the lap of a boy-page —a *foot*-page in the most literal sense—who, seated on the floor in front of him, kept gently chafing the royal toes and ankles during the whole meal, and folding them, ever and anon, in his white mantle, as if to keep them warm.

But all this was in strict accordance with the most revered laws of Howell Dha, the great Welsh law-giver, who had ordained that "the foot-bearer shall hold the king's feet in his lap, from the time that the king reclines at the board till he goes to rest, and shall chafe them with a towel; and during all that time he shall watch that no harm befalls the king. He shall light the first candle before the king, and shall eat of the self-same dish from which the king takes his food."

Just behind the Lion King stood his "pen-bhairdh," or chief poet—the poet-laureate, in fact, of this wild court—who, in reply to his master's appeal, broke forth, after a brief but stirring prelude on his harp, into a wild song of triumph over the success of their recent forays into the land of their Saxon foes :—

"When the Lion of Wales roars from Pen-maen-mawr the sheepfolds of Hereford tremble, the Saxon churls mutter with pale faces, 'Where shall we hide?'

"Stronger is the white mantle of the Cymry, with a stout heart behind it, than the steel breastplate of the sons of Hengist, covering a faint spirit.

"Who is like unto Gryffyth, the son of Llewellyn, the Lion King, unmatched in war? His spear falls swifter than the dew of June from the reed-grass the battle melteth at the glance of his eye.

"When we marched through the pastures of the Salopians [Shrewsbury men] we made widows of all the Saxon wives.

"Long shall Saxon orphans tell of the coming of the Cymry, when the red mouth of the fire devoured hovel and tower together.

"The maiden smiles as she wades the summer-dried brooklet, the winter torrent sweeps away horse and rider. Warriors of Powys-Land, ye are the winter flood! Gryffyth, son of Llewellyn, thou art the foam of its highest wave!"

And then this wild chant, the fierce energy of which fired even Kenneth and Fillan, who but partly understood it, changed all at once to a soft, sweet, plaintive cadence, as the bard, with one of those sudden turns in which the Welsh poets of that age delighted, transported his hearers' fancy to the Lion King's far-off mountain home :——

" Far away on the mountain top sits watching for his coming the bride of Gryffyth the king.

" Fair is she as the first flush of dawn on the snowy hills. Wherever she sets her foot milk-white flowers spring up beneath it.

" The child looks up in her face and asks, ' When comes my father home ? '

" Bright is the sun around them, gaily sparkle the gold bracelets on their wrists, strong and well-guarded is the hold of Pen-y-Dinas ; but all seems empty, for *he* is not there ! ''

There were tears in the eyes of the grown-up children as the bard ended ; and the visible softening of the wild faces, which but a moment before had been all aflame with fierce excitement at the stirring words of the war-song, amply attested his triumph.

King Gryffyth himself, visibly touched by this un-expected mention of his fair Saxon bride, daughter of Earl Algar of East Anglia, whom he had wedded a year or two before, unclasped a heavy gold bracelet from his bare arm, and gave it to the poet, saying courteously,——

" So sweet a harp should be strung with naught less than golden wires ! "

Macduff and his friend were seated a little apart from the rest, pretty close to the king, but not actually by his side; for Gryffyth, knowing how prone were his proud and fiery chiefs to resent the least appearance of a slight, took good care to avoid even the suspicion of honouring the two stranger youths above *them*. Thus it befell that, as he turned from addressing the bard, the Lion King saw Kenneth's eye fixed on him with a look of eager, boyish interest.

"Seem I so outlandish to thee, friend of my kinsman, that thou look'st so hard at me?" asked Gryffyth with a pleasant smile, for he had already taken a great liking to this bold northern lad, whose frank, fearless nature was so much akin to his own.

"Deem me not so ill-mannered, King of the Cymry," said our hero, "as to stare at thee as at some outlandish sight. I did but look at yon twisted chain of thine as being like one whereof I heard a goodly tale not long ago."

"I would fain hear that tale," cried the king eagerly, for a good story was as much prized as a good song in that bookless age. "Shall I bid my bard lend thee his harp?"

"I thank thee," said Macduff hastily; "but even were I a poet—as I am none—it would ill befit me to let my voice be heard after such a minstrel as he. Nay, rather suffer me to tell my tale in plain words even as I heard it."

"So be it," said the king; "and my chaplain here"—pointing to Father David, who had attended as usual to bless the food—"will interpret for such as understand not thy northern speech."

And Kenneth began his tale—a fair sample of the strange jumble which that age made of all classic history :—

"Many a year ago there came over the mountains into Italian land a huge host of Saracens, who had heard much of the riches of Rome, and were minded, like godless heathens as they were, to plunder the holy city, and burn our father the Pope in his own palace. And wherever these Saracen unbelievers came—Gauls they called themselves—they burned chapel and shrine, and snatched the sacred vessels from the altars, and parted the consecrated robes among them, and carried off the images of the holy saints, saying profanely that they must be weary of standing there so long, and that it was time for them to move.

"Terrible they were to look on, these Saracen Gauls, huge in stature, misshapen, and marvellously ill-favoured, some with long ears like horses, others with goats' feet and hairy skins like bears. But ugly as they were, they loved to prank themselves in silver and gold; and all their chiefs wore even such a twisted gold chain as thou, O king, art wearing now."

"What!" cried Gryffyth angrily, "dare Paynim dogs wear the ornaments of Christian kings? St. David! if e'er I meet a heathen so adorned, it shall go ill with him! But let that be, and on with thy story, young chief, for in sooth 'tis a brave one."

"But when they of Rome heard thereof," went on Kenneth, "they came forth to meet them, under the banner of a valiant knight who was their captain, fearing naught, for well they wist that Heaven itself would be against the sacrilegious Paynims who had blasphemed its saints and robbed its altars.

"When the two hosts came front to front, there stepped forth from the Saracen ranks, like Goliath of old, a mighty giant, who in a terrible voice defied any of the knights of Rome to single fight, on the condition that they whose champion was overthrown should yield to their foes, and own themselves vanquished.

"Then came forth a young Roman esquire, Titus Manlius by name, and offered to meet this heathen boaster, saying that he who fought in God's cause

"It is I who should thank thee for saving the life
of my child."

could never be overthrown. But the old general looked doubtfully on him, for he was but a youth, and small and slim withal"—here all eyes turned instinctively to King Gryffyth's small, slender figure —"and he seemed but a sorry match for the mighty Paynim.

"Then said the youth right boldly, that in his own strength he was indeed no match for this giant, but that greater than the might of the body was the might of the spirit, and *that* he could not lack, fighting in a holy cause. And the old knight blessed him, and said to him, 'Go!'"

A quick indrawn breath hissed through the silence, betokening the listeners' universal and absorbing interest.

"When the giant saw this slim youth come forth against him he laughed scornfully, and thrust out his tongue in mockery, knowing himself to be proof against all weapons, by the power of those black spells which Mahound [Mohammed] taught to his worshippers. But he wist not that Esquire Titus's blade had been blessed by the Pope himself, and that against *it* no magic availed aught.

"The Gaul whirled aloft his mighty mace, one stroke of which could shatter a solid rock, but ere the blow could fall, the Roman flew in under it, and

with his keen sword smote him through breastplate
and through breast, that he fell down and died.

"When the heathen host saw their champion fall
they cried out and fled in dismay, and they of Rome
pursued and smote them with a great slaughter.
And Titus Manlius took the gold chain from the
neck of his dead foe, and offered it up in the Church
of the Blessed Virgin, where it lieth to this day;
and forasmuch as in the Roman speech such a
chain is called 'torques,' the old general dubbed him
knight by the name of Sir Torquatus, or 'He of the
Chain.'"

All the listeners heartily applauded the tale; and
King Gryffyth, pleased with its implied compliment
to himself, asked eagerly,—

"From whom gat'st thou yon goodly tale, Chief
Kenneth?"

"From a good monk of St. Benedict's rule, of St.
Aidan's Priory, nigh to Chester. He, coming up
when my comrade Fillan was fallen sore sick by the
way, and I wist not what to do, helped us to the
priory, and cared for us there as had we been his
nearest kin; and there we abode a whole month, till
my comrade was sound and whole of his sickness.
And when we departed thence, Father Ailred—so was
this kindly monk named—gave us directions for the

way, and good store of food thereto. May God reward him for it ! "

" And since he hath showed such kindness to my kinsman," said the king heartily, " if ever I fall in with him, I will reward him too."

CHAPTER XIV.

CLUTCHED BY A MONSTER.

A TINY, fair-headed child, laughing and clapping her little hands in glee as she rolled to and fro on the green sward of a deep hollow between two huge gray blocks of moss-clad stone; other stones as grim and massive, strewn far and wide over the steep slope, like the ruins of some ancient fortress; and a pale gleam of sunshine above, lighting up spectrally, as it broke through the gray sullen sky, the bones of the dead city.

A dead city indeed it was that clung to the wild mountain-peak of Pen-maen-mawr, with the sea outspread below it on one side, and the whole expanse of north-west Wales on the other. The superstition of the age held it to be the work of giants or demons; and even now the best antiquaries are still at fault as to its builders and the date at which it was built.

But, whoever those unknown architects were, they did their work well.

Four successive walls, nearly eight feet thick, girdled the hill-top; and though gapped and crumbled by time and storm, they were still formidably strong.   These grim ramparts stood fully eighty yards apart, and in the spaces between clustered numbers of those strange circular hovels, mere overgrown beehives of stone with a single narrow opening for door, window, and chimney, which Julius Cæsar's keen eye noted as characteristic of the "British savages" of his time, and which still survive in the Hottentot and Zulu kraals of our own day.

In the centre of the space enclosed by the innermost wall towered the massive stones of one of those famous "Druid circles" preserved for us in Stonehenge, and in the midst of this ring lay the broad flat slab on which the grim priests of that gloomy creed were wont to slay the human victims of their ghastly sacrifices.   Far down the hillside were seen the remains of other walls, showing what a mighty circuit this city of the dead must once have had; and the ponderous fragments of these defences, piled along the rocky ledges, and ready to fall at any moment, would of themselves have been a formidable obstacle to the boldest assailant.

Such was the scene that lay before the eyes of Fillan of Lochaber as he stood watching the gambols of King Gryffyth's little daughter Gladys, who was already a special pet of his, though neither he nor any one living could then have guessed how strangely his fortunes were one day to be entwined with those of that child and her mother.

The mother, however, was much less to his liking than the child, and not without reason. Queen Aldyth, or Ældwyth, Saxon woman as she was, had nothing high or great in her weak, shallow nature, and cared little for the brave and true-hearted warrior who had wasted on her all the deep devotion of his strong, simple heart. In truth, she cared for no living thing but herself; and even the young Scot's indulgent eyes could read plainly in her beautiful, heartless face that mean and miserable selfishness that made her the most despicable figure in one of the grandest periods of English history.

For a stranger like Fillan to be thus at home in Pen-y-Dinas (Head of the City), as this weird stronghold of the past was called by its present owners, was a privilege to be highly valued, for few of the native Welsh themselves, save Gryffyth's personal followers, could boast of having even approached its walls, much less set foot within them.

Nor, in truth, were there many, even among the boldest of them, who would have cared to do so if permitted, so deep and universal was the awe inspired by that mysterious spot. If their king chose to live in such a place, well and good; as for them, they had no mind to venture near a fortress that was the work of no earthly hands.

But to the two young Scottish nobles, who had never seen anything like it before, this dreaded maze of ruins was a perfect playground, and they were never weary of clambering over the mouldering walls, peering among the fallen stones, crawling into the hive-shaped dwellings, or leaping from boulder to boulder along the lower slopes, ever on the lookout for any sign of the buried treasures or unburied bones of the giant builders, in whom they believed as firmly as any Welshman in the whole district.

On these explorations they were always accompanied by little Gladys, whom they carried by turns, and very often by her half-brother, Prince Caradoc, Gryffyth's son by his first wife—a fine boy, just emerging from childhood, whose handsome face wore that look of strange melancholy which the belief of the age held to forebode an early death.

But on this special morning—a fine day in the

early spring—Fillan and Gladys had it all to themselves, for Kenneth and Caradoc had gone down to
the valley with King Gryffyth himself.

The young Scot, having romped with his tiny
pet till she was fairly tired out, had at last left
her snugly ensconced in a sheltered spot, while
he, never dreaming that any harm could befall her
there, went off to inspect the interior of a low,
massive, half-ruined tower a little to the right.

But it contained neither a hoard of enchanted
gold, a skeleton giant, a magic word engraved on
the wall, or any other marvel, and the young
wonder-seeker was just coming out again dis-
appointed, when he suddenly caught sight of something that made his bold heart stand still.

Barely a hundred yards away, and much nearer
than himself to poor little Gladys, was gliding over
the open space, stealthily and silently, right toward
the unconscious child, the long gaunt body of a
huge gray wolf !

From the spot where the young Scot stood Gladys
was not to be seen ; but that the wolf had either
seen or scented her was only too clear. Softly and
noiselessly as the monster crept on, its gaping jaws
and quivering tongue and the murderous gleam
in its narrow, greenish-yellow eye told but too

plainly that it was aware of the presence of this unlooked-for prey, and bent on seizing it forthwith.

Fillan flew rather than ran toward the savage beast, with a shout that made the air ring.

At the sudden appearance of this new foe the beast's native cowardice made it pause for a moment, and quick as thought Fillan snatched up a heavy stone as he ran, and hurled it at the wolf with the force of a giant.

A sharp howl told that it had not been flung in vain, and the momentary check given to the fierce brute by this sudden blow enabled the lad to throw himself, with one frantic rush, between the wolf and its prey, while his right hand felt for the trusty dirk that had never failed him yet.

But alas! in that headlong dash the weapon had fallen from its place, and he stood wholly defenceless as the furious beast sprang at his throat.

Not a moment did Fillan hesitate. With his bare hands he flung himself on his terrible foe, and man and brute went down together in a whirl of flying dust, while the screams of the frightened child shrilly answered the shouts of the Scot and the fiendish yells of the monster.

Fillan was already a redoubted champion, but for once he had fairly met his match, and more;

and but for the disabling wound inflicted on his foe by the heavy stone, the combat would soon have been over. The wolf was one of the largest of its kind, and maddened with pain and hunger; and Fillan, weary from his late exertions, and spent with that last desperate rush, was in poor case for such a death-grapple.

Over and over they rolled, the wolf struggling frantically to tear itself free and fix its teeth in Fillan's throat, while the young athlete threw his whole strength into the strangling clutch on the brute's lean, sinewy neck, on which his life depended.

But such a strain was too exhausting to last. Already he felt his grasp beginning to give way; and as his own strength failed, the wolf's struggles grew more and more furious. The hot, rank breath steamed in his face—the foul, yellow, cruel eyes glared into his—the huge body pressed with stifling weight on his chest—one moment more, and then—

Something flew by him like the whiz of an arrow; there was a dull thud—a hoarse, gasping growl; the deadly pressure relaxed, and then, dimly as in a dream, he saw the wolf lying dead by his side, with a Welsh javelin buried in its body, and over him bent anxiously the bold, firm face of King

Gryffyth himself, behind whom stood Kenneth and Caradoc.

"Art thou hurt, lad?" asked the king quickly, as he raised the panting Scot.

"Not I," gasped the bold lad, as he began to revive from the strain of that death-grapple; "but I owe thee my life, king, and I would I could thank thee as I ought."

"Thank not me," said the Lion King, "but rather thank God, who sent me hither just in time. It is I who should thank thee for saving the life of my child, which I prize far above mine own."

And while Caradoc and Macduff praised and congratulated Fillan, the grim king tenderly soothed and caressed his poor little trembler, who, not yet recovered from her fright, turned away her head with a shudder from the sight of the dead wolf, and clung closer to her father, hiding her still pale and tearful face in his sheltering breast.

When King Gryffyth recalled that feat in after-days, he probably thought of it—so far as he thought of it at all—merely as the killing of a stray wolf that had attacked his guest, a matter so ordinary as to be hardly worth mention. What he had really done was to alter the whole future of Britain.

For some time after this adventure the two young

exiles led, for them, a very quiet life; for in the council held by the king at Curig Cogh it had been decided, to the deep chagrin of the younger and hotter chiefs, to risk no further fighting with the Saxons, and go quietly home with the spoil: then, having thus thrown their foes off their guard, to wait till the Saxon forces now gathered on the border had dispersed to their homes, and, when the coast was clear, to swoop on the defenceless Hereford Marches with fire and sword.

As a matter of course the king invited his Scottish guests to join this destroying raid, just as a modern host might ask his friends to a picnic; and equally as a matter of course, both joyfully agreed. But while they were eagerly awaiting the time fixed for the foray, came to their mountain fastness from the outer world from which they were so strangely cut off some news in which both lads were deeply interested.

The storms of early spring had driven into the mouth of the Conway river, not far from King Gryffyth's stronghold on Pen-maen-mawr, a Flemish merchant-ship, homeward-bound from Ireland. Her crew were kindly received by the hospitable Welsh, and her captain entertained by the king himself in the coast town of Caer-Gyffin, close to the spot now occupied by the Conway railway station, and by the famous castle which is still one of the marvels of North Wales.

To requite this unlooked-for kindness—for he had fully expected to be robbed and ill-used, if not murdered as well—the Fleming set himself to amuse his royal host with all the news he had picked up on his way; for in truth, in an age when letters and newspapers were not, the gossip of traders, pilgrims, and strolling minstrels was the only means by which news could be carried at all.

In his talk the captain mentioned a name interesting to all who heard it, and doubly so to the young Scots—the name of Harold, Sigurd's son, of Norway. Of the great sea-king's recent feats he had plenty to say; and Harold's deeds, marvellous enough in any case, certainly lost nothing in the telling.

When blockaded in a narrow inlet by his Danish foes with a fleet of twenty-three vessels, the Norse leader had steered his one ship right through the hostile squadron under cover of a thick mist; and being challenged in passing from one of the Danish ships as the fog began to melt away, he ran her down and sunk her, making his escape while the other vessels were picking up her struggling crew.

Then, in sheer boyish love of adventure, this bold rover had landed on the coast of Wend-land (now East Prussia), and had penetrated to a strong woodland fortress of the heathen natives, in which a famous local idol was worshipped with human sacrifices. Harold stormed the fort, knocked down the hideous image, hacked it to pieces before the very eyes of its dismayed worshippers, burned idol and temple together, and then fought his way back to his ships in the teeth of all opposition.

After this he went on to the coast of Russia, and landed amid the shaggy woods of which some traces still exist around the modern palace of Peterhof. Here he was kindly received by the wild tribesmen of the district, whose hospitality he repaid by undertaking to hunt down a huge bear that was greatly distressing them with its ceaseless ravages. Having tracked the beast to its lair, he reached its den by climbing a precipice that most men would have thought quite unscaleable ; and then, with no weapon but the dirk that he held in his teeth during the ascent, attacked and slew the dreaded beast.

In the struggle, however, Prince Harold was so fearfully mangled by the monster's teeth and claws that no one expected him to survive ; and when he did recover after all, his admiring men gave him the well-earned nickname of Hardrada (the Hard), by which he is still known in history.

But the great sea-king's latest feat, as told by the Fleming, left even these marvels far behind.

The previous winter had been such a hard one that the narrow strip of sea parting Denmark from Sweden (now known as the Sound) was frozen right across, thus freeing the Danes, as *they* thought, from any risk of being molested by Harold Hardrada's ever-restless ships for several months to come; and the Danish king, having gathered his chiefs around him at Helsingör, or Elsinore, then the capital of Denmark, was holding his Yule feast, in full confidence of being safe from attack, in that grim old sea-fronting castle which, if quaint old Saxo Grammaticus speak truth, was once the abode of a certain Prince Hamlet, of whom we all know something.

" Health to Harold, Sigurd's son ! " cried the Danish king mockingly ; and all his guests echoed the toast with scornful laughter as he raised the brimming horn to his lips. " Health to him, and may he have a merry Yule, where'er he be ! "

" I thank thee, Magnus, Olaf's son, of Denmark ! " said a deep voice from the end of the hall ; and there, towering in the doorway, stood Harold, Sigurd's son, himself, helm on head and axe in hand, his

giant form seeming vaster yet in the fitful torchlight, and behind him glittered the weapons of his
sturdy crew.

"Health to Denmark, and to all brave men!" said
Harold, as, striding up the hall, he took the horn
from the startled king, and drained it to the last drop·

"What wouldst thou?" asked King Magnus,
taking in at a glance, like the cool, practical man
that he was, the very awkward dilemma in which
he found himself. He and all his guests were
quite unarmed, and between him and his warriors
below stood fifty stout Norse rovers, armed to the
teeth.

"Food for my men and me," said Hardrada
coolly, "for, having marched over the frozen sea
from Sweden, we be hungry as hawks."

"Over the sea from Sweden?" echoed all the
company with one voice, for such a feat startled
even them.

"Food shalt thou have, and welcome, for thou
hast taken such a lucky grip of me that I trow
I can scarce refuse," said the Danish king, with
a laugh of boyish good-humour at his foe's superior
cleverness, as he glanced at the armed giants who
hemmed him in. "Sit down and eat, thou and
thy men."

In a trice Harold and his crew were quite at home among their foes, for these simple, overgrown children knew no medium between slaying a man on the spot and welcoming him like a brother, and young Magnus felt his heart warm to a reckless daring so like his own.

That night Hardrada and his men slept fearlessly in their enemies' fortress, and on the morrow, before the wondering eyes of King Magnus and his Danes, they marched back over the frozen sea to Sweden.

"I ween thou wilt now be doubly proud of thine adopted brother, Chief Kenneth," said the Welsh king, as the tale ended, for he had long since heard the whole story of young Macduff's friendship with the famous sea-king.

"Ay, truly," cried the Scot heartily; "and ere long I hope to pass over the sea and join him, since there is no home for me now in my own land, and go a-sailing with him as we purposed long ago."

"Art thou already weary of me, then, lad?" said Gryffyth reproachfully, for by this time the wild northern youth and the wild southern man were like an elder and a younger brother. "Methinks thou may'st at least bide with me till we have looked the Saxon in the face once more."

"That will I, I vow it on the edge of my dirk!"
cried Kenneth warmly, using the most solemn pledge
of good faith that a Scottish warrior could give.

But he had cause, ere long, to repent of that hasty
pledge.

Barely three days later a passing pilgrim brought
word that Kenneth's father, the great Thane of Fife—
of whom our hero had heard nothing since the thane's
marvellous escape from Macbeth's vengeance in
the previous summer, had found refuge with Earl
Siward of Northumbria, and that Malcolm Canmore,
the slain King Duncan's eldest son, was there too, in
the hope of persuading the earl to aid him in over-
throwing Macbeth, and regaining his kingdom.

At this news Kenneth and Fillan looked meaningly at each other.

"Had I known of this before," said the former,
at last, "I had set forth this hour to join my father,
but my word is passed to Gryffyth, and keep it
I must. Howbeit, lad, the word for thee and me
will be 'Northumbria ho!' as soon as this expedition
is over."

Little guessed poor Kenneth what the end of that
expedition was to be. But it is not given to man
to read the future; and well for him, in truth, that
so it is.

CHAPTER XV.

A FIERY PRISON.

ALL Hereford was in an uproar. Every narrow, crooked street of the quaint old town swarmed with hurrying figures, and faces livid with fear or black with rage; and from the country round more men kept flocking in, and more and more, rudely armed with hatchets, clubs, knives, bill-hooks, hunting-spears, or huge iron forks, and looking as stern and gloomy as men might be expected to look who knew that the next hour might see them mangled corpses or homeless beggars, and their wives and children dragged away to a slavery worse than death.

The straggling market-place of the town was already crowded to overflowing, and all eyes were bent on the tall dark tower that rose high above the mass of peaked roofs and overhanging eaves, and quaintly-carved gables round it, crowned with dancing flames by the blaze of the beacon-fire which,

repeating the alarm signal that had run from tower
to tower along the whole Welsh border, told to the
Hereford Marches that King Gryffyth and his wild
men were in the field once more to burn and slay
without pity.

The women and children had been hurried off to
the cathedral, the only refuge where they could
possibly be safe—if, indeed, even it were safe from
these savages—in the death-grapple that was just
about to begin. At the minster gate they met
Bishop Leofgar himself, no longer in his priestly
robes, but in full armour—his mitre replaced with
a helmet, and his crosier with a heavy battle-axe.

"Marvel not at mine array, my children," said he,
as he raised his hand to bless them. "I wot well
that the Church's rule forbids her servants to mingle
in war, but I trust God will pardon the shepherd
who takes arms but to save His flock from the wolf."

And all this while the broad, smooth stream of the
Wye shone like gold in the peaceful beauty of a
glorious summer sunrise, and the green leaves made
a pleasant murmur in the fresh morning breeze, and
the birds sang blithely on the trees that overhung
the winding river, as if neither sin nor sorrow had
ever darkened that spot since the world began.
But far to the west and north the clear blue sky

was blotted with rolling clouds of smoke, showing where many a happy home lay desolate, and many an honest hard-working man who had lain down in peace and plenty had been startled from his sleep to find himself and his family houseless, beggared fugitives, with death in its worst form at their heels. Such is "glorious war!"

High on the summit of the great minster tower, in the glory of the sunrise, stood a small group of gray-haired monks, who, as they watched with anxious eyes the surging smoke-clouds that marked the advance of the destroyer, raised their thin, trembling voices in a very appropriate psalm :——

"Plead my cause, O Lord, with them that strive with me, and fight against them that fight against me. Take hold of shield and buckler, and stand up for my help. Draw forth also the spear, and stop the way against them that persecute me; say unto my soul, I am thy salvation."

But all at once the quavering chant faltered, and then ceased altogether; and one of the singers, pointing downward, said, with a look of unconcealed dismay,——

"The men of blood are upon us, brethren; may God have mercy on us, for vain is the help of man."

Then, through the terrified silence that followed,

rose, clear and unfaltering, the firm voice of a white-haired monk in their midst, whose countenance was conspicuous among all those troubled faces for its calm and fearless composure.

"Be of good cheer, my brothers, and let not your heart fail because of them. They are but men, and He who is on our side is stronger than they."

"Ah, thou speakst ever boldly, brother Ailred," said an old monk by his side peevishly; "but wouldst thou not thyself wish now to be back in that quiet priory of thine by Chester town?"

"I would wish," replied the monk-historian in a tone of mild but firm rebuke, "to be wherever I may best serve the cause of Him whose servant I am. Let us now get us down in haste, and bestow in a safe hiding-place the altar vessels and the church's offerings, that so, if these godless men break in on us, they may find naught to plunder."

Down the stair he hurried as he spoke, and, stranger and passing guest as he was, there was a nameless something in his look and tone which all the rest instinctively obeyed as they would have obeyed the bishop himself. Their task done, the anxious watchers hurried up once more to their post on the tower, from which they beheld a strange and fearful sight.

Had the Saxons been content to await the attack in the town itself, they would almost certainly have been victorious, for in those narrow crooked streets the Welsh could not bring their superior numbers to bear, and exposed as they would be to a ceaseless shower of missiles from the windows and housetops on either side, must have fought at a grievous disadvantage.

But the fatal rashness that was to ruin all England on the field of Hastings twenty years later showed itself here on a smaller scale, with equally baneful results. The bold Englishmen, furious at the sight of their blazing homes and plundered goods, no sooner saw the plunderers fairly within reach than, forgetting all prudence in their burning eagerness for action, they quitted their strong position and rushed out to give battle in the plain.

This was just what the wily Gryffyth had wished and expected; and as they came charging on, he made a show of falling back before them, till he had lured them well out into the open field. Then suddenly the terrific yell of the Cymrian war-cry rent the air, and a huge mass of white-clad warriors swooped on the Saxons' unprotected flanks from either side, while the king himself, with a body of picked men, burst upon them in front.

To the dismayed watchers on the minster tower

it seemed as if all were over with their countrymen, for amid that great host of white-clad foes the struggling handful of dark hide coats and leathern jerkins looked no bigger than a solitary clump of bushes on a snow-covered moor.

But the sturdy Saxons, like true Englishmen, never knew when they were beaten, and sternly closing their ranks, they set their faces toward the town, and forced their way stubbornly onward through the swarm of leaping, striking, howling figures around them.

Many fell by the Welsh javelins, and the Cymrian host dashed and surged around their fast-thinning ranks like waves bursting on a rock; but at last the dogged English hardihood prevailed over the wild Celtic fury, and the Saxons, though sorely diminished, regained the town once more.

Here the fight was more even; for when crowded together in those narrow, winding lanes, where a score of resolute men might have held at bay a whole army, the great numbers of the Welsh were a hindrance rather than a help, and the hopes of the gazing monks on the tower were beginning to rise again, when a thin wisp of smoke was seen to curl up from one of the houses, quickly followed by another and another.

"They have fired the town," groaned one of the older monks despairingly, "and all is lost!"

All was lost, indeed. The long heat and drought of summer had made the planking of the houses as dry as tinder, and the fire, once kindled, flew from roof to roof, and from wall to wall, till the whole town was one red and roaring blaze.

The defenders were thus driven forth pell-mell, and it would have gone hard with them had not the Welsh victors just then begun to scatter in quest of spoil, fearing to have their booty snatched from them by the advancing flames. This respite enabled the Saxons to fall back to the minster, where the bishop was already at the head of his vassals, with a number of stout lay brothers, and not a few of the monks themselves.

But their respite was a very short one. Hardly was the last man at his post when the Welsh war-cry broke out all around them, and the wild warriors came rushing and roaring up to the rude palisade of pointed stakes that was the usual Saxon idea of fortification.

Men who were wont to scale precipices with no aid but twisted roots, thorn bushes, and inch points of rock, were not to be checked by a stockade barely twice their own height. Clambering over each other's shoulders, hacking the stakes in two, or even bearing them down with the sheer weight of their rush, the wild men came bursting in like a wave, their war-yell rising louder and fiercer than ever, as the answering Saxon shout of "Holy Cross! Holy Cross!" grew fainter and fainter.

At the minster gate the English made their last stand, and heartened by the stirring words of brave Bishop Leofgar, who, wounded as he was, cared nothing for his own peril compared with that of "the sanctuary of God," held their own for a few moments by sheer dogged courage, even against such fearful odds.

But all their heroism was vain; for now the Welsh, furious at this prolonged resistance and the slaughter that it had cost them, fired the outbuildings all around, while at the same moment a slender tongue of flame was seen to curl up from the timber roof of the minster itself, which had been kindled in turn by the ceaseless gusts of sparks from the burning town.

"This is no work for thee and me, comrade Fillan," said Kenneth to his friend, who, amid all this maddening hurly-burly, had never left his side for a moment. "I will have naught more to do with it. To face our Saxon foes I am ever ready,

but I will have no hand in burning the church of
God ! "

" Howbeit, let us forward," cried Fillan, " if haply
we may save some of these good monks from rough
handling. I bear a good will to them all for the
sake of yon kindly Benedictine who tended me in
my sickness at the priory by Chester town."

Forward they hurried in the track of a band of
shouting Welshmen, who came rushing on as if
meaning to storm the church itself, the gate of which
had just been shut and barred behind the wounded
bishop and the two faithful monks who carried him.

But where *were* they, and whither were they going ?
Through the blinding, stifling smoke that shut them
in—filling their smarting eyes, and making every
breath a convulsive gasp—nothing could be seen but
the glare of fresh flames springing up all round
them, and hemming them in on every side.

Even the men just in front of them could no
longer be seen, and their presence was only made
known by their cries of terror and bewilderment
as they stumbled on, choking and half stupefied,
through the thick black smoke-clouds that billowed
around them.

Bold as they were, the young nobles began to
feel dismayed. They were pent up in a perfect

prison of fire, from which there seemed to be no escape; for the pitch-smeared timbers of the out-buildings were all ablaze around them, and the western end of the minster itself was beginning to burn fiercely.

But all at once a gust of wind rent the veil of smoke, and showed them a gap in the ring of flames that hemmed them in. To the left, a small wooden shed, protected on either side by a thick tree, was still unkindled, and by slipping between it and one of its guardian trees they might make their way unharmed out of this deadly maze.

One moment more and they would have done so; they would have rejoined their comrades, and all that was now at hand would never have been. But just as they got up to the shed they heard a harsh voice say within,—

"Tell me at once where thy church treasure is hid, or I'll pierce thine eyes with my dagger point!"

"Lay not such a sin on thy soul, my son," said a clear, mild voice, the sound of which made our heroes start; "for though thou shouldst hew me limb from limb, never will I give up to robbers the money that belongeth to the poor of God!"

At that voice the two Scots sprang in like wild cats, and found a fierce-looking Welshman stooping, dagger in hand, over a prostrate monk, in whom Fillan at once recognized the good old man who had nursed him in the priory.

"Father Ailred!" shouted both lads at once, darting to the spot.

The enraged savage had already raised his dagger to make good his horrid threat; but ere he could strike, a crushing blow from the pommel of Fillan's sword beat him down to the earth as if a mountain had fallen on him, and the young heroes bore the helpless monk gently forth.

But hardly had they left the building, when Kenneth, who was foremost, was startled by a fearful crash overhead; there was a burst of flame that seemed to set the whole air on fire—another crash louder than the last—a stunning shock—and all was a blank.

CHAPTER XVI.

THE MYSTERIOUS MONK.

"WHERE am I?" asked young Macduff feebly, as his senses came back to him.

"Thou art safe, my son, and likely to do well, God be praised, though I had well-nigh given thee up for dead at the first," said the kindly voice of Father Ailred, who was seated by his side.

"And what of my comrade Fillan?" inquired the young Scot anxiously.

"He sleeps; wake him not," replied the monk warningly, as he pointed to another pallet near Kenneth's, on which lay the young chief of Lochaber with his arm bound up. "Nor must thou, my son, speak yet awhile, for thou art still too weak; I will tell thee all thou wouldst know."

Kenneth was quite willing to obey, for he felt strangely sick and dizzy, and his head, which was covered with a thick bandage, ached as if from a heavy blow.

He lay still, therefore, and listened attentively while the monk told how the flying fragments of a blazing beam, fallen from the burning church, had struck down Kenneth and his friend; how he himself, left unhurt as if by miracle, had succeeded, he knew not how, in dragging them back into the yet unburned shed; but the circle of fire kept narrowing round them, and he was beginning to despair of saving them, when unlooked-for help came.

A fresh Saxon force, which had just come up to the rescue, fell suddenly on the scattered and unprepared Welsh, and put them to flight with great loss. Ailred called to his aid some of the victorious English, by whom the two lads were speedily borne to a place of safety, and then soldiers and townsmen alike flew to quench the flames that were devouring the minster.

In this they were quite successful, with the aid of a furious torrent of rain that came just in the nick of time, and Father Ailred's joy at the saving of the church was heightened by the news that the bishop's wounds were not dangerous. Little did the joyful monk foresee that the half-burned church and the wounded prelate had only escaped for a time, for ten years later another of King Gryffyth's destroying forays laid the cathedral in ashes, and brave Bishop Leofgar perished in a vain attempt to defend it.

The leader of the Saxon victors—no other than the Earl of Hereford himself—was not long in hearing of the two Scots who had been saved from the fire, and lost no time in asking who they were and what brought them thither. To these queries Father Ailred, who could not have told a lie to save his life, replied by frankly owning that the two lads had come with King Gryffyth's host, and that one of them was the Welsh king's relative by marriage.

The earl heard with marked satisfaction that he had in his hands a hostage of such importance, and at once gave orders that the Scots should be well treated, but closely guarded, till it could be settled how best to turn their capture to account.

While Ailred was speaking, Kenneth's keen eye roved watchfully round the small, bare chamber, which seemed a monk's cell of the ordinary type, probably belonging to that part of the monastery that had escaped the fire; for when, not long after, Father Ailred rose to depart, Macduff could hear plainly through the open door the rush of the river below, as if they were actually over it.

Our hero replied heartily to the old monk's kindly farewell, and followed his vanishing form with a look of affectionate admiration; but he was far from guessing that this obscure monk would be remembered long after he himself was forgotten, and that the rude Latin chronicle on which Ailred was then engaged would one day form part of the history of England.

The crash of the closing door awoke Fillan, who stared around him in bewilderment; and Kenneth, who was almost himself again by this time, hastened to repeat all he had learned from the friendly monk. This done, they talked over the position, in low tones and in their native speech, for a murmur of voices and clank of arms told that Saxon guards were within earshot.

They soon agreed that, for the present at least, escape was out of the question. Their door was barred and guarded; the opening that served as a window was too narrow to let them pass; and even had the chance of escape been a better one, they were in no plight to take advantage of it—Kenneth being still weak and dizzy, and Fillan having one arm disabled.

After all, they were, on Ailred's own showing, quite safe for the time, and their buoyant spirits were but little disturbed by what might befall later.

Having made a hearty meal on the coarse but

solid food brought them at nightfall by a sturdy Saxon soldier, the brave lads prayed their evening prayer as usual, and lay down to rest as quietly as if they were at home.

With the morning came Father Ailred again to speak a few kind words to them, and to look at their hurts, which he pronounced to be doing well.   He told them that nothing had yet been decided as to their fate, but that some decision would probably be arrived at that very day, and as soon as it was he would let them know.

After such an announcement it may be imagined with what impatience the eager lads watched for his return.   But afternoon waned into evening, and evening began to darken into night, and still there was no sign of him.

It was already all but dark when they heard his voice outside, and yet—*was* it his voice after all ? It sounded wonderfully like it; but there was a difference of some kind, though they could not tell what.

" Give this food to the Scots, my sons, for they must needs be a-hungered," said the voice, as if to the guards at the door; " and here is somewhat to mend your own cheer.   Meet it is that ye should fare well this day, for it is a Sunday and the Feast of St. John."

A moment later in came the warder who usually brought their food (a big, good-humoured, heavy-looking Saxon) with a huge platter of meat and a rye loaf, which, he said, the good Father Ailred had brought for them himself.

"Comes he not to speak with us?" asked Fillan quickly.

"Nay, for he went speedily forth, as one in haste."

And the worthy Saxon went speedily forth himself, as one in haste to get his share of the good cheer brought by the monk, whatever it might be.

This confirmed our heroes' conviction that the visitor was not Father Ailred, but some one playing his part. But what could be the motive of such a masquerade, and who was he that had undertaken it?

Neither of them could guess; but, after all, there was time enough to think about that. The first thing to be done was to have their supper; so they fell to with a will.

About an hour later, as near as they could guess, during which time the cell had grown quite dark, the door, as if of itself, suddenly and silently opened.

No step had been heard outside——no challenge from the men on guard——no sound of unbarring the door. But open it was, and in the doorway stood—as they could see by the dim light of the hanging lamp without—a tall, shadowy form in a monk's robe and cowl, the latter completely hiding its wearer's face, and making the whole figure seem more like a flitting shadow than a living man.

Superstitious like all men of that age, the Scots were more than half inclined to believe that this ghostly stranger who had entered so mysteriously could be no being of this world; and Kenneth was on the point of bidding him be gone in Heaven's name, when the spectral intruder spoke,—

"The peace of St. John be with ye both. Rise and follow me."

It was the same strange voice which was and yet was not that of the good monk Ailred, and the lads hesitated, recalling the tales they had heard of unwary mortals who, beguiled away by evil spirits under various forms, had been torn in pieces or carried off bodily. But seeing that he wore the garb of a monk, which no demon could be supposed to do, and that, as he uttered the saint's name, he neither fell down writhing nor vanished in a flash of blue fire, they began to feel somewhat reassured.

"Rise quickly and come," repeated the visitor. "This hour—nay, this moment—ye must fly, or it will be too late. Father Ailred, being suddenly called hence, hath bidden me tell ye that the Saxons are minded to remove ye both from this place on the morrow and put ye to close prison. This night must ye escape then, and all is ready for your flight; wherefore come, and tarry not."

So saying, he glided ghost-like to the door of the cell. The two young nobles followed at once, for to their bold spirit the mere mention of "close prison" was more than enough. Convinced at last that this man meant well to them, and that in passing himself off as Father Ailred he had taken the readiest means of gaining access to them, they were now quite as eager to be off as he seemed to be himself.

At the door our heroes were startled to see their Saxon warders lying motionless on the earth; but the heavy breathing of the unconscious men told that they were only asleep. The three or four empty flasks beside them fully explained their condition; but the shrewd lads saw at once that those few flasks could never have overpowered the iron heads of these giants, and that the liquor must have been drugged.

As they passed, their guide took from the nearest soldier's belt a heavy key, with which he opened

a door at the end of the passage. The coolness
of the outer air came freshly on the young Scots'
heated faces; and scrambling at the guide's heels
down a steep, narrow path, they saw a faint glimmer
of water below, and felt themselves handed aboard
a boat, which at once shot away into the darkness.

Down the stream they went at a rapid rate; and
this voyage in utter gloom along an unknown river,
piloted by this mysterious and ghostly guide, and
propelled by rowers whose very faces they could
not see, had in it something so weird and unnatural
that they almost thought it a dream, and half expected to awake suddenly and find themselves back
in their cell once more.

But they were not left long in darkness. The
moon was already rising, and her light, streaming over
the tree-tops that stood black and ghostly along the
high, shadowy bank above them, showed that they
were on a light boat rowed by two men, and steered
by their unknown rescuer himself, which, going with
the current, flew down the "whirling Wye" at a
marvellous rate.

By the time they had shot past the spot where
the Arrow from the north-west, and the mingled
waters of the Frome and Leddon from the north-
east, came rushing into the broadening stream of

the Wye, the young fugitives began to think themselves safe from pursuit, and Kenneth thought it time to ask their strange pilot whither he was carrying them.

" Rather should I ask, my sons, whither ye would wish to be carried," said the stranger courteously ; " for now can no pursuit overtake us, and ye are free to go where ye will."

" If that be so," said young Macduff, " the nighest road to my father in Northumbria is the road that best suiteth my comrade and me."

" Art thou Earl Siward's son, then ? " asked the monk quickly, with an emphasis which amply showed that the query had a special interest for him.

" Not so," said Kenneth ; " but my father is his friend and his son's friend, and even now a guest at his castle."

The other was silent for a minute or two, as if pondering the last words ; and then he said, with the slow, grave earnestness of one who had thought well over what he was saying,—

" Methinks, then, it were best for ye to land on the east side of the river when we reach Monnowmouth [Monmouth] ; for thence may ye right easily make your way over Severn stream into Wessex, where, I trow, it will not be long ere ye can join some company of cheapmen [traders] bound northward, or a train of pilgrims faring to St. Cuthbert's shrine. And now, I rede [advise] ye, take a sup of this cordial to warm your blood, for the night it waxeth chill."

What the friendly pilot called cordial seemed to the lads very like ordinary red wine; but it had a sweetish, sickly taste quite new to them, which the stranger ascribed to a flavouring of spices.

Not long after this both began to feel drowsy, and their guide advised them to lie down and have a nap, kindly giving them a warm cloak to cover them, and promising to wake them when the time came. They did not need to be told twice, and were soon fast asleep, though even in dreams they were dimly haunted by the exciting adventures of the last few days.

All at once a rough shake broke Kenneth Macduff's slumbers, and he looked up with a start of amazement.

Was he dreaming still? Surely, surely this confused whirl of wild forms, strange dresses, and grim swarthy faces, all eyes and teeth, that flitted around him in dim lantern-light, could only be the phantoms of a nightmare.

Alas! it was no dream, but a terrible reality, as

a rude clutch on his arms and limbs too fully showed him.

River and banks had vanished, and they were now lying amid a dim waste of open water which seemed to have no end. A second glance told the dismayed Scot that their boat was alongside of a long, low vessel of outlandish build and rig; and even as he looked, he saw his friend Fillan hauled aboard the strange craft, bound hand and foot.

One moment more, and the strong hands that were pinioning Kenneth's own wrists and ankles had done their work, and he felt himself, in turn, half dragged and half carried on to that sinister-looking vessel, amid a hoarse clamour of voices in an unknown tongue.

Then the hideous truth burst upon the ill-fated lad in all its horror. Their treacherous guide had betrayed them to a Moorish corsair, and he and Fillan were being carried away captive to be sold as slaves.

CHAPTER XVII.

IN THE HANDS OF PIRATES.

THERE was great stir and bustle in the old town of Waterford, then a Danish colony and the capital of a Danish king.

A Moorish ship from Spain—which was then, and for many a year after, in the hands of the Saracens— had just come in, and was lying off the town with a cargo of slaves, who were about to be landed that the king might take his pick of them as usual, after which all the rest were to be sold to the best bidder; and the town folk were flocking to bargain over this peculiar merchandise as men of our time flock to a sale of pictures and rare books.

Nor had King Ranald Sigtryg's son of Waterford far to go to inspect the newly-arrived goods, for the long, low wooden shed that served him as a palace stood right on the quay to which the slaver was moored, just at the foot of the huge, massive round

tower of dark-gray stone, which, built by his pre-
decessor Ranald Iron-beard forty years before, was
then known as the Tower of Dundory, but which,
under the name of Reginald's Tower, any tourist to
Ireland to-day may see for himself.

Perched on its summit, the Danish watchman who
had announced the coming of the slave-ship could
command a noble view.

To the south-east lay outspread, for many a mile,
the smooth, bright waters of that splendid roadstead,
which was then, as now, one of the finest harbours
in Europe. A little beyond the town the headlong
Barrow came glittering and glancing down from its
far-off hills to pour itself into the broad brown
stream of the Suir, and rush together with it to
the sea.

Just below him lay King Ranald's half-built
timber church of the Holy Trinity, and behind it
the quaint little Danish town, with its rude cabins of
tarred planking, and the mud hovels of the native
"thralls" whom the king's big, fair-haired, hard-
hitting warriors had captured in their ceaseless raids
on the territory of their Irish neighbours.

Far to the west rose, blue and dim, the Commeragh
Mountains; and away to the north-east surged up,
ridge beyond ridge, the border hills of Wexford.

Due north of the town extended, far as the eye could reach, that great panorama of green slopes and purple moors and dark thickets and glittering streams which was one day to be called County Kilkenny; and over all hung the soft pearl-gray Irish sky.

And now the landing of the slaves began; and out came King Ranald to look at them—a hale, hearty, bright-eyed old gentleman, whose broad, ruddy, jolly face looked as little as possible like that of a man who could burn whole districts into a blackened waste, and butcher every living thing in them, as he had done, and was still doing, again and again and again.

But it was from sheer love of a good bargain, and not because the coming over of a slave ship from England to Ireland was anything unusual, that the king and his men took so much interest in it; for, hard as our age may find it to believe such a thing, that same England which has since, thank God, been a chief mover in putting down the slave trade all over the world, was then carrying on a systematic slave trade of her own, not in negroes, but in Christian Englishmen—ay, and women and children too—whom their countrymen deliberately sold into bondage.

So completely, in fact, was this traffic in human flesh a recognized feature of Saxon England that no less a person than Dame Thyra, the first wife of the great Earl Godwin himself, is chiefly remembered in history for the prominent part that *she* took in it. And, to make all this even worse, the chief agents of this infamous carrying trade were Saracens, the very people whom Saxon churchmen and Saxon laymen alike were wont to denounce as "infidels" and enemies of God.

"Be these, then, all that ye have on board?" asked the king, as he walked round the thirty slaves who had just been landed, to see which he would like best to have for his own—the "duty" paid in this primitive custom-house on all goods brought ashore.

"All," said the Moorish captain without hesitation. To a brother Moslem this staunch Mussulman would no doubt have acted with true Mohammedan good faith; but a falsehood told to a "Christian dog" was in his eyes not only excusable but fully justified. What he had just said, in fact, was a downright lie; for there were still two captives left on the Moorish bark, who would have seemed to the king's critical eye worth all the rest put together.

Since their capture, Kenneth and Fillan had been in no plight to attempt an escape, even had it been

possible: for during their passage of St. George's
Channel, the rough sea had paralyzed all their
energies with the clutch of sea-sickness; but as the
ship got into smoother water under the lee of the
Irish coast, our heroes began to revive, and set themselves to consider their situation.

They easily guessed that the pretended monk must
have been one of the professional slave-dealers who
abounded along the ever-disturbed border-line of
Wales, buying Welsh captives from the Saxons, or
Saxon captives from the Welsh, as the fortune of
war might turn. It was, no doubt, at his suggestion
that the Moorish bark had been lying where they
found her, in the Bristol Channel, off the mouth of
the Wye (Bristol being then, as it was six centuries
later, the chief port of the English slave trade); and
by the care taken to entrap and secure them, it was
plain how valuable they were thought to be, and how
little hope they had of escaping the sleepless and
covetous vigilance of their captors.

But with returning strength and recovered power
of action—for their bonds seemed to have been
slackened so much that they easily got their hands
free—their determination revived to achieve their
freedom at any risk.

Through a small square opening in the timber

wall of their prison they could see land looming high and bold to starboard, and this, judging from the time that had passed since they set sail, could be nothing else than the coast of Ireland; and as the nearest Irish port was Waterford, to it they were probably bound.

Waterford, to be sure, was a Danish town, and the Dane was, as a rule, no friend to the Scot; but the bold lads preferred the risk of being knocked on the head by Christians and Northmen like themselves to remaining in hopeless bondage among heathen savages—for such the Moors of Spain, in reality one of the most civilized races then existing, were held to be by all Christendom.

They decided, then, that as soon as the Moorish bark lay to off the town, they would, in the ensuing confusion, break out, if possible, from their place of confinement, leap overboard, and swim ashore. If they succeeded, they would at least have a chance of life; and if they perished—well, they would at least die *free*.

But in this calculation, as they were soon to learn, they had greatly underrated the shrewdness of their crafty and rapacious kidnappers.

Just as the two lads, peering through the cracks in the mouldering planking of the small "deck-

house " that was their prison, had made out land
on both sides, and rightly guessed that they were
running up the long, straggling, landlocked inlet of
Waterford Harbour, the clumsy door was unbarred,
and in came two of the Moors, each with a huge
wooden bowl brimful of a warm black liquid.

The thirsty lads drank eagerly; and as they did
so, the Moors, seeming to pay no heed to the fact of
the captives having freed their hands, much less
taking the trouble to bind them again, went out
without a word, barring the door behind them.

The young Scots were much refreshed by their
draught, though not a little puzzled at the aromatic
odour and strange taste of the unknown drink, which
was quite new to both.   And well it might be, for
this was the first time they had ever seen, much less
tasted, *coffee*, which Britain was not to know for nearly
six centuries to come, though it was already in
common use with the Moorish masters of Spain.

But they had not much time to think of it; for
hardly was the last drop swallowed when an overwhelming drowsiness and torpor, or rather a kind
of temporary paralysis, began to steal over them both.

They were still conscious of their intention to
escape—they still knew that their hands were free,
and that they had only to unbind their feet; but, as

in a troubled dream, they felt powerless to stir a finger or even utter a sound, and ere long both lay extended on the floor of their prison in a slumber so deep and heavy that it might well have been mistaken for death.

When they awoke all was dark; but though they could see nothing, the vessel's motion told them that she was going swiftly on, despite the gloom.

Then, all at once, Kenneth started half erect with a cry of dismay.

"Treachery, Fillan! I see it all now: yon liquor was drugged!"

"Like enow," said his comrade, yawning, "for my head is yet heavy as a pine beneath the winter's snow. But what of it? we have slept well, and when we get to Waterford—"

"We shall see naught of Waterford this time, I tell thee," broke in Macduff impatiently. "Seest thou not that while we slept these rogues have touched at Waterford, done all their business, and set sail again? And now are we being carried out to sea once more!"

For a moment Fillan stood mute with dismay; and then he called out,—

"Howbeit we have not yet reached the open sea, for lo! a light on this side."

Kenneth looked, and he too saw, through the opening above, a pale spot of light high in the air, but evidently not a star.

"Good; there is hope yet!" cried he, with an air of relief. "Let us free our feet quickly, and then will we try if we can break forth of this wolf-trap."

But just then in came two of the Moors with a lantern—not, however, the same two—and Kenneth had barely time for a hasty whisper to his friend ere the corsairs made fast their bonds once more, so tightly as to leave both lads utterly helpless. Then they withdrew, one of them saying with a grin,—

"Insh' Allah [please God] the Christian curs will not easily get free now."

But the worthy pirate might have been less confident on that point had he seen what took place as soon as his back was turned.

Kenneth's whisper had warned Fillan to follow his example by clenching his fists and stiffening his muscles to the utmost when his arms were bound; and so, when the tense muscles relaxed, the cords that tied them relaxed also.

Both lads at once bent themselves backward and then forward, expanding their chests and straining their arms to the utmost, and continued to do so, heedless of the pain it cost, till they felt the pressure of their bonds slacken. At last Kenneth succeeded in wriggling one hand free, and with it freed the other; and then he unbound Fillan, and a little chafing of their numbed limbs soon restored their full power of action.

This done, Macduff's next move was to feel along the roof for a strong iron hook that he had seen there, meant no doubt to support a hanging lantern. He soon found it, and set himself to work it out of the wood, which, the planks being much decayed, proved easier than he had dared to hope.

Here, then, was a first-rate tool for his intended prison-breaking; and now the only thing left to settle was in what way to use it.

His first idea was to pierce a hole in the planking of the door, and remove the bar that held it; but a moment's thought told him that this bar, held fast at both ends as it must be, could not be removed from the inside, and an instant more suggested to him a far better plan.

Feeling in the dark along one wall of the deck-house, while Fillan groped along the other, Kenneth soon discovered that one of the crazy planks was so loose at the top that, if loosened at the foot as well, it might be easily removed, and leave a gap wide enough to let them pass out without much trouble.

To work he went at once; and as if on purpose
to make his task easier, the moon, which had risen
very late, came streaming at that moment right into
their cell, giving him ample light for his work.

But even with this aid it was a long task.   There
being but one tool for them to use, they could only
work one at a time; and the rude implement with
which they were labouring blistered and cut their
unpractised hands again and again.

Nor, unluckily for them, were these by any means
the only hindrances with which they had to contend.

Had they dared to break off the lower end of the
plank chip by chip, it would have been a far quicker
job; but this was just what they must not do, lest the
scattered splinters, and the hacked appearance of the
plank itself, should draw the attention of their jailers,
who might come in at any moment, and so ruin all.

Thus they were forced to use the spike as a
gimlet, and bore a number of holes through the
mouldering wood, as close together as possible, so
that at last the lower end would be quite cut through,
and the plank, though still remaining in its place,
could be removed whenever they thought fit.

But though they laboured by turns, the cramped
posture unavoidably assumed by the one who was
working was too intolerable to be borne for more

than a few minutes at a time; and moreover, with all their caution, it happened at last that a splinter of wood broke off with so loud a crack as to make their hearts die within them, for it seemed impossible that the noise should not have been heard by some one of the Saracen crew.

For a long time they lay crouching in motionless silence, holding their breath to listen; but at last, as they neither saw nor heard anything to alarm them, Kenneth took the spike from Fillan, who had been working at the time of the mishap, and was about to take his turn of labour, when a sound of steps and voices was heard coming right toward the door.

Quick as thought, Macduff thrust the iron hook back into its place in the roof, lest its disappearance should beget suspicion. Then he and Fillan hastily retied their ankles, and, winding the cords round their wrists so as to appear undisturbed, lay down on the floor as if asleep.

With all their haste, however, they would not have been quick enough to escape detection had the pirates entered at once. But luckily for them, one of the Moors, in the uncertain light, stumbled over some obstacle, and fell sprawling on his face; the other paused to help him up, and even this delay of a few seconds made all the difference.

In came the Saracens, happily without a lantern this time, for the moon gave light enough for their purpose; and thus there was little risk of their detecting the slight traces of work which, with all their care, our heroes had not been able wholly to avoid.

Stooping over the pretended sleepers, the Moors tried the cords and found them firm, the lads having cunningly grasped one end in their hands so as to make sure of its not giving way. But the shrewd Macduff, rightly judging that it would appear suspicious should he seem unconscious of being thus shaken, gave a slight start, and muttered some half-articulate words like a sleeper suddenly aroused. The savage corsair dealt him a kick by way of apology for disturbing him, and, complimenting him with the title of "Christian dog," withdrew again with his comrade.

The young Scots waited a long time ere they dared to move, lest their jailers should return; and when they at last ventured to rise, it was only to cast off their bonds once more, for the resuming of their work was not to be thought of. The moon had set, and any attempt to labour in the dark would do more harm than good; and all they could do was to wait till dawn came to aid them.

But when it did come, it showed them a startling sight.

Fillan, climbing on to his friend's broad shoulders, managed to get his face right through the square window-hole above them, and looked round eagerly to see where they were; but hardly had he done so when he leaped back to the ground with an irrepressible groan of bitter disappointment.

All their toil, all their courage and shrewdness, had been utterly in vain. The Irish coast lay five or six miles behind them, and they were right out in the open sea, on their way to hopeless bondage!

CHAPTER XVIII.

A STRANGE SAIL.

FOR one instant even the buoyant spirits of the two brave lads were crushed by this terrific blow; and the sudden hardening of their bright, fresh faces told that, in their utter desperation, they held death itself preferable to the earthly hell of Moorish slavery, and that the only thing left for them to do now was to fight till they were killed.

But just then came hoarsely to their ears a confused clamour of many voices from without, in tones of unmistakable excitement and alarm.

Plainly enough, something had happened which was causing no small disquiet to the pirate crew; and it behoved our heroes to find out what that something was as soon as they could.

Nor did they take long to do so. Scrambling up again on to his comrade's back, and peering through the opening, Fillan espied a strange vessel to windward, which, having seemingly just issued from

behind a headland a little to the north-east, was now
bearing down on them before the morning breeze.

Whoever she might be, the stranger was clearly
a craft of no ordinary speed ; and a general turning
of faces and pointing of fingers towards her among
the pirate crew told plainly that she was the cause
of their uneasiness.

The strange sail neared them fast, and as she did
so Fillan's keen eye soon saw by her build, her rig,
and the glittering line of shields along her gunwale,
that she was one of the northern warships which
every coast of Western Europe then knew to its cost.

" Thank God ! " said young Macduff fervently, as
his friend, leaping down again, told what he had
seen. " Yon men, if they be from Norway or Denmark, will fly at these Saracen rogues as the hound
at the wolf ; and we must be ready to take our part
along with them."

" That will we blithely ! " cried Fillan ; " it is for
liberty and life ! "

Just then, as if to give them the means of carrying out this resolution, Kenneth caught sight of a
small Moorish dagger that had no doubt fallen from the
belt of one of the pirates as he stooped over them to
examine their bonds, and which, having slipped into
a crack of the floor, had escaped their notice till then.

Joyfully did Kenneth clutch this new weapon, with which he assailed the loosened plank so vigorously that it was soon quite detached and ready for removal.

By this time the warship had come so near that the pirates could see her crew preparing for the attack. The shields were snatched from the gunwale, a spear gleamed in every hand among those who stood behind the rowers, and the steersman, who managed the helm with admirable skill, was seen to be driving her right at the pirate, evidently meaning to "run on board" of her, and either sink or capture her by boarding.

On came the warship in all her power and splendour, glittering and glancing in the cloudless glory of the sunrise——her shining oar blades flashing and falling in perfect time, her huge white sail swelling out to the breeze, and the gilded serpent that formed her prow seeming to dart its open mouth and quivering tongue at the doomed pirate.

There was a moment's pause of terrible silence, and then came a quick, sharp order from the pirate captain, and at once a shower of Moorish arrows went whizzing at the assailant, and fell rattling on her deck.

Several of the rowers were hit, and the helmsman

was struck twice; but the helmets and mail coats of these northern giants had repelled far more formidable weapons than the light cane arrows of the corsairs. The slender shafts snapped like twigs on the trusty armour, and no one was a whit the worse.

But the pirates were not to be so easily disposed of as their foes expected, for the corsair too had her best man at the helm.

Twice the *Serpent of the Sea* darted at her as the wolf-hound at the wolf; and twice a skilful turn of the pirate's helm let her glide harmlessly by. As she slid past, the bold Northmen, in turn, hurled their spears with amazing force; but the wary Moors kept close, and but one man was seen to fall.

Ere the warship could make a third effort, the distance between the two vessels began to increase visibly; and the Norsemen ground their teeth with rage at the thought that the corsair might slip by them into the open sea, and thus, being their match in speed, escape them after all.

But just then came a sudden and startling interruption.

It happened that the loosened plank was in that side of the deck-house that faced toward the stern, and through the crack Kenneth had keenly watched the Moorish helmsman's manœuvres, and had seen to what they tended. In a moment he thrust the pirate dagger into his friend's hand, with a few whispered words; to which Fillan replied by an assenting nod, and then, as cautiously and noiselessly as possible, they removed the plank and crept forth.

Ere the startled helmsman, astounded at their sudden appearance, had time to speak or move, Macduff struck him down with one blow of the iron spike. Then seizing the helm, the bold Scot jammed it hard down; and ere the pirates, from whom all this was hidden by the deck-house, could tell what had happened, round swung the corsair "broadside on" to the attacking warship.

Crash! the assailant struck her fair and full, the sharp prow keeping firm hold of her side; and at once a wave of armed men burst with a mighty shout over the slaver's deck.

Meanwhile Fillan had not been idle. In the general confusion he had scurried up the mast as nimbly as the wild cats of his native mountains, with the Moorish dagger in his teeth. Quick as thought he cut loose the huge, heavy sail, which in its fall buried at least a dozen of the pirates in its thick folds. Most of the others were flung from their feet by the collision, and thus the Norsemen's onset took them at a complete disadvantage.

Seizing the fallen helmsman's short sword, Kenneth was at once in the thick of the fray; and Fillan, sliding down the mast, was at his side in a trice, dagger in hand.

All that followed was like a troubled dream. A confused whirl of flashing steel and wild faces, coming and going like the phantoms of a nightmare—a deafening din of trampling and slashing and shouting, the Moorish war-cry of "Allah Ackbar" (God is victorious) mingling with the mighty "Aoi!" of the Norsemen, for which our modern hurrah is a poor substitute—and then Macduff felt a sudden shock and a sick, dizzy faintness, and the last thing he knew ere he became unconscious was a strong arm supporting him, and a deep voice saying,—

"What? my brother Kenneth Macduff of Scotland? Well met, lad!"

And the voice that spoke was that of his adopted brother, the renowned Prince Harold Hardrada of Norway!

"Where am I?" asked young Macduff, as he opened his eyes once more.

"Aboard Prince Harold's *Serpent*, and a fine craft she is," said his friend Fillan, who sat by him with a bandaged head and a bound-up arm. "Good cause have we to thank God, lad, for such a deliverance;

for rather had I died than lived on in bondage to the unbelievers."

"Even so say I too!" cried the other, with grim emphasis.

"In truth thou hadst well-nigh done so, comrade," said the Lochaber lad gravely; "never thought I to hear thee speak word more, when I saw thee go down beneath the stroke of yon scimitar."

"I have been wounded, then, belike?" said Kenneth, becoming dimly conscious of a dull pain in his head, and a thick bandage that encircled it.

"That hast thou, in very deed; and I have had a taste of the steel too, as thou seest. These Saracen blades bite deep, but it is not to be thought that the infidel dogs should be able to stand against Christian men. Hadst best sleep while thou canst, lad, for thou seem'st sore foredone; and ere long will Harold of Norway himself come to talk with thee."

Sure enough, when our hero awoke some hours later, the first object that met his eye was the giant form of his old friend "Hard Harold," who, softening his mighty voice to a cautious undertone, bade him heartily welcome.

"Nay, no thanks, lad," added he quickly, as Kenneth tried to express his gratitude; "it is I who should thank thee, for it is all through thee and thy

comrade, and by no deed of me or mine, that yon
Saracen rogues were entrapped after all, even when
they had well-nigh escaped us."

"Made ye good prize out of her?" asked his guest.

"Ay, truly, we found rich booty, and stowed it
aboard our own craft; but the ship herself, which I
would fain have saved—for, Saracen though she were,
she was a goodly vessel—hath dived down into the
sea like any whale. I feared that so it would be
when I saw our prow smite her ribs so sharply, for
my *Serpent* striketh not in vain; and yon sleight of
thine with the Saracen's helm gave her a goodly
chance. Of a truth, when yon rovers made ye captive they did as ill a turn for themselves as the
dragon that would have swallowed St. Margaret, and
burst himself in the doing of it! And now, brother
Kenneth, wot'st thou whither I am bound?"

"Wherever perils are to be met, I trow," said
the Scot.

"Right," said the young sea-king, with sparkling
eyes; "and the Saracen dogs with whom we have
dealt this day will be but as a sop to stay our stom-
achs till the full meal be ready. I am bound, lad,
for the Midgard Sea [Mediterranean], for men say
that in Sicily the Christian folk be sore holden down
by the infidels; and I am minded to aid them, and

to win bright gold and brighter fame in warring with these servants of Satan. How say you, lad? wilt come with me?"

"Small need to ask that, I wot," said Kenneth proudly; "thou know'st *me*."

"That do I," cried the other heartily, "and better comrades at need than thou and Fillan could I wish none. Bide thee still awhile, and anon I will come to thee again."

"But tell me, I pray," said our hero, as the sea-king rose to depart, "hast thou still with thee Sweyn Eric's son, Biorn Hare-foot, and Nine-man-Mord?"

"Aha! thou hast not forgotten them, then?" said Harold, with a pleased smile. "In sooth they are yet with me, and shall be while they and I live; for well saith our northern rede, 'Old wine and old friends are ever better than new.' I will go tell them what thou say'st, and right glad will they be, I trow, that thou so bear'st them in mind. But, now I bethink me, thou wilt see Eric's son for thyself ere long; for he, thou know'st, is the leech [doctor] of my crew, and it is his charge to tend all who are hurt or sick."

In fact, half an hour later, a cautious step made the Scot look up to see the shaggy white beard and hard face of old Sweyn himself, who greeted with a rough smile "the lad that had not forgotten him."

"Thou art a good lad," said he warmly, "to remember old Sweyn all these years. Care not for this scratch of thine; I tell thee it will be naught. The best medicine for a warrior, lad, is this good sea-air thou art breathing; and never trust me if, in a few days' space, thou art not whole and sound as the best of us."

In fact, our hero's wound, though painful, was less severe than it looked. His thick cap had turned the blade that would else have cloven his skull, and he had been prostrated by the great loss of blood from his hurt, rather than by the hurt itself. As Sweyn, Eric's son, had said, the pure sea-air and his own fine constitution wrought wonders for him, while old Sweyn's untiring care did the rest; and but a few days later he was able to come on deck with Fillan, whose hurts were happily slight, and to receive a hearty welcome from the whole crew, more especially Biorn Hare-foot and Nine-man-Mord.

The two lost no time in showing him and his friend every part of their new ship, in the building of which they had both, as well as Sweyn, Eric's son, had no small share.

And certainly the *Serpent of the Sea* was well worth looking at. More than eighty feet from stem to stern—strong, light, sharp-prowed—just broad enough in the beam to steady her without making her heavy—she was the very model of an eleventh-century man-of-war. High forecastle, high poop, capable of being defended separately; for in those days a ship's forecastle was a castle in the most literal sense, and often held out long after the rest of the ship was taken. Twelve oars a side in the waist, which was open but for a raised gangway on either side, along which the sure-footed Norsemen could run to and fro even in a rough sea. Cabins fore and aft, large enough to hold not only the crew, but all their stores, their armour, and, more important still to these born rovers, the spoil taken in war. A row of shields along either gunwale, shining in the sun like plates of silver. One short, strong mast, and one huge sail—for the warship of that day was merely a big row-boat—over which waved Harold Hardrada's " raven banner," one day to be so terribly famous under the too apt name of " Land-Eyda " (Earth-Waster).

To the unused eyes of the young Scots, each new detail of this model ship seemed more wonderful than the last; and they were as much pleased with her, and as proud of belonging to her, as the Norsemen themselves.

The weather was beautifully fine, and as they flew

south with a fair wind over the bright summer sea, with the cloudless blue of the southern sky overhead, our heroes felt the buoyant thrill of reviving health and strength pulsing more vigorously, day by day, through every nerve and vein.

Filled with the delight of being once more among friends, and having escaped that hideous bondage the mere thought of which made them shudder, the brave lads would have been perfectly happy but for the haunting thought that Kenneth's father must still be mourning him as dead, and that they had no means to let him know the contrary.

But when Prince Harold heard of this trouble he made very light of it.

" Bide but till we pass the Niorva-Sund [Strait of Gibraltar], and it shall go hard but we find in Sicily, or in Italian-land, some pilgrim or cheapman bound for England who can bear tidings to the Jarl Macduff that thou art safe and well. Be assured thy father will not call thee ' niddering ' [good-for-nothing] when he shall hear that thou art sailing under Harold Hardrada's banner ; and when thou comest back to him with store of good red gold and the renown of a man and a warrior, I trow he will be better pleased with thee than he would hadst thou bided deedless at home ! "

Our hero renewed his intimacy not only with Sweyn, Mord, and Hare-foot, but with all the rest of the crew; but his special crony was old Saemund, the eldest seaman aboard, who had steered the warship inshore to rescue him from the wolves on the memorable day of their first meeting.

The terrible Bay of Biscay was already past, and Kenneth was seated on the poop one evening admiring the far-extending panorama of the beautiful coast of Portugal, even more picturesque then than now, from the addition of a tall white Moorish tower or a quaint Eastern mansion every here and there.

"I ever deemed, lad," said Saemund's deep voice behind him, "that thou wouldst one day come with us over the swan's bath [the sea]; and no better captain couldst thou have, I trow, than our Harold, Sigurd's son."

"No, truly," cried the Scot warmly; "he is the bravest man I have ever known."

The old warrior's face quivered as if in sudden pain, and he said in an altered voice,—

"The bravest man *I* have ever known was an old man who had never handled weapon in his life."

"Ay; how chanced that?" asked Macduff eagerly, guessing that this strange utterance must preface a tale of no common interest.

" Heard'st thou ever how I became a Christian ? "
said the old man, looking fixedly at him.

" Never," said the Scot, turning to him with an
air of marked interest.

" Hearken, then, for 'tis a tale worth hearing,
though few there be that know it.   Three-and-thirty
years agone we Norsemen, with certain Swedes and
Danes to aid us, harried East Anglia with a mighty
host, to avenge the blood of our brothers whom the
Saxons had murdered by treachery, setting on them
unawares in every town of England from the one sea
to the other.   Thence came we over Thames stream
into the land called Kent; and there we sacked Can-
terbury town, and burned it with fire.

" But whereas we weened to have found much
booty, we found none at all ; for the churchmen were
ware of our coming, and had hid all the church
treasure.   Then were we wroth, and bade drag into
the hall, where we feasted with Tall Thorkell, our
chief, the Archbishop Ælfheah himself——for he fled not
with the rest, but bided firm at his post——and we set
him in the midst, and bade him give up the treasure
to us if he loved his life.

" Quietly and fearlessly he stood facing us as we
threatened, as if our spears and axes were but blades
of grass.   Methinks I see him now, with his long

white hair and his clear blue eye, a calm smile on his face, and in his eye a look that the boldest of us could not meet.

"'Heaven forbid,' quoth he, right boldly and firmly, 'that I should give up the money of God's poor to heathen robbers. Not one penny of it shall ye touch, though ye slay me where I stand!'

"I tell thee, lad, the stoutest of us stood as if spellbound, so uncanny did it seem for this frail old man in robes of peace, who stood in our midst unarmed and helpless, to defy us thus to our faces. But on a sudden one cast an ox bone at him, and smote him on the face therewith, that the blood sprang.

"Then it was as if we all went mad at sight of blood, and the spirit entered into us that bids men tear and slay like wild beasts. We hurled at him ox hoofs and bones and horned skulls, till he was well-nigh buried, and so sore hurt that he sank to the earth, with his white hair all dabbled in blood.

"Then as he lay I saw his lips move, and these were the words he spake,—

"'Father, forgive them; they know not what they do.'

"Then a great pity came over me, and I vowed that he should suffer no more torment; and with that I heaved up my axe, and smote him that he died!"

Here the old warrior's voice was choked by an emotion of which he had no cause to be ashamed; and Kenneth felt tears start to his eyes as he listened.

"Then," resumed Saemund, "some murmured at me, saying I had marred their sport. But the more part, now that the deed was done, seemed amazed and dismayed, as men waking from an ill dream; and one by one they slunk away without a word, till no man was left in the hall save I alone.

"'This is a man, and like a man he hath died,' said I to myself, as I stood looking down on him; 'wherefore I will do him what honour I may, for in truth he hath well deserved it!'

"With that I wrapped him in his robes, and took up the body to bear it away, being minded to bury it with mine own hands. But as I bare it forth I met certain of his own monks, who had come to our camp to seek him; a right gallant deed, I wot, for the sheep to come thus into the wolf's den.

"They took the body and bare it away, and dug the grave with their own hands, and laid him in it; and I stood by silent and sorrowful.

"Then all but one turned their faces from me as were I a leper, or one who had fled from battle, for well I wot they held *me* alone guilty of the old man's blood, and deemed that I only had so ill entreated him.

"But there was one face among them on which I saw neither hatred nor loathing, but much pity instead. A good and a gentle face it was, that might move a man to tell out all his heart, with full assurance of being understood. Moreover, he was a young man like myself, and I deemed that he would judge me less harshly than these graybeards who had outlived their hot youth, or who, belike, had never been young at all.

"So I stepped up and craved a word with him, and told him all my tale, even as I tell it thee now.

"'Be of good cheer, my son,' said he gently; 'inasmuch as yon blow of thine was dealt in mercy, it shall be counted unto thee for good, and not for evil. Even were it otherwise, who am I to gainsay the forgiveness that he who is gone spake to thee and thine with his dying breath? Say not men that even among the very soldiers who slew our Lord Himself there were some who in after days were called by His name, and drank the cup of martyrdom for His sake? Go in peace!'"

"But as he turned to depart there came upon me a great longing, I wist not why; and I threw myself at his feet—I, who had never yet knelt to mortal man—and thus I spake :—

" ' Teach me thy faith, father, for it is stronger than all our weapons. Thor and Odin, the gods of my fathers, can make men fight hard and die hard; but He who can make a frail old man that has never fought braver than Odin's own warriors must needs be the mightiest of all. I would fain learn more of thy " White Christ;" and if He will have me I will be His man, and He shall be my Master!'

" ' Amen!' quoth the monk; ' as thou say'st, so shall it be. Come with me; but first give me thy hand, and promise—for I know a Northman's word is to be trusted—that never more wilt thou slay any man save in fair fight!'

" I promised as he spake, for he had said he could trust me, and after that he led me away, and talked much with me, not proudly nor harshly, but as friend with friend; and at the last I took baptism at his hand—for I would have taken it at none but his—and when we parted he blessed me, and bade me remember Brother Ailred of—"

" Ailred?" broke in young Macduff eagerly; " Brother Ailred of St. Aidan's Priory, hard by Chester town?"

" Aha! thou know'st him?" cried the Norseman.

"The better for thee, then, for there lives not such a man of God 'twixt the four seas of Britain; and fain would I see his face once more.

"As for the slain archbishop, they call him St. Alphege now, and men say that in London town hath been builded a goodly church in his honour. To that church will I give rich offerings, if I come back safe from this voyage of ours; and I trust he hath forgiven me, for brave men harbour no malice, and he was the bravest man I ever knew."

CHAPTER XIX.

FIERY MESSENGERS.

"HAST thou seen aught of movement, brother Habib, in the camp of yon Christian curs?"

"That have I, in very deed, friend Ali: the infidels are spreading nets, as if they were minded to make captives of the larks and sparrows!"

The speakers were two young Arab warriors, who were looking down into the besieging camp that half encircled the small Sicilian town of Ponterotto, the quaintly-carved battlements and Eastern gateways of which, as well as the white dome and tall, tapering minarets of the Mohammedan mosque that rose above them, showed it to be one of the many places still held by the Saracens—though their supremacy was now drawing to a close—in that oft-contested island over which had swept so many successive waves of conquest.

But there was no sign of war in the quiet and

beautiful panorama on which, from their well-guarded walls, the two young soldiers looked down. So far from that, the whole scene had the aspect of a holiday fair.

Behind the white tents of the camp, which made so goodly a show in the bright morning sun, the tender green of the vines that clustered over the sunny slopes contrasted very prettily with the dark glossy leaves of the orange trees in the hollow below, through which a tiny stream went dancing and sparkling to the sea. Away at the upper end of the valley stood out, huge and dark and massive against the deep rich blue of the cloudless summer sky, the broken arches of a half-destroyed Roman bridge, whence the town took its name of Ponterotto (bridge-broken).

Even the besiegers' camp was far more like a gaudy May-day pageant than a centre of strife and blood. In the brilliant southern sunlight gay flags waved, helmets shone, spear and axe flashed and sparkled. Men were bustling to and fro, fetching water, cooking food, eating fruit, cleaning their weapons, contending with each other in wrestling, leaping, and running, or, as the Saracen watchman had said, spreading nets as if for bird-catching.

" Ill off indeed must the infidels be for food if they

are fain to trap small birds to eke out their store,"
said Ali mockingly.

"No doubt they find it easier to crack sparrows'
bones than the walls of our town!" cried Habib,
echoing his comrade's sneer with a loud, scornful
laugh; "and, in truth, it is fitter work for such
faint-hearts to storm birds' nests than to face the
swords of the Faithful."

"Speak not so lightly, ye sons of folly!" broke in
the stern voice of an older man behind them; "look
that your own hearts be strong, ere ye call them
faint-hearts who made the Asinari stream run red
with the blood of the true believers. There is one
in yon host, I trow, whom—brave as ye think yourselves—ye would rather see from these walls than
stand face to face with!"

Old Osman plainly thought it needless to tell
them of whom he spoke; and, in fact, at that very
moment, as if to add double force to his ominous
words, a mighty figure, towering a full head above
the tallest of the stalwart forms around him, was
seen to come striding along the front of the hostile camp, and to look keenly for a few seconds
at the besieged town, after which he turned and
disappeared.

"Behold him!" said Osman, with grim emphasis.

"Will ye call *him* faint-heart, and say that he is only
fit to rob birds' nests?"

"Nay; truly he hath slain too many of our people
for that," said Ali, in a tone of savage and reluctant
admiration. "Mighty is his arm to smite, and
among all the swords of the Faithful there is none
that can match his. May vultures pick his bones,
and dogs defile the grave of his father!"

"Would he were himself a believer, and leading
our hosts to war!" cried Habib, in a nobler spirit;
"for if he fought as well for the true faith as he
hath done against it, soon should we be lords of all
lands betwixt the inner and the outer sea. Many
a valiant warrior have I seen, but never one like the
Son of Hardness, whom his own people call Harold
Hardrada."

In fact, though less than two years had passed
since the great sea-king's raven flag first showed
itself in southern waters, his name was already
a terror to every Saracen, and a joy to every
Christian, through all Sicily on one side, and the
whole coast of North Africa on the other.

And well might it be so. The feats that he had
already achieved, partly by sheer reckless daring
and partly by the shrewdness with which that
daring was so strangely combined, were so marvel-

lous that his Moslem foes could account for them only by the supposed power of magic; and what with his real abilities as a conqueror, and his imaginary ones as a wizard, the fiercest pirates of the Mediterranean trembled at his very name.

Harold's first Sicilian exploit would have seemed impossible to any other man; and, just because of its seeming impossibility, it succeeded.

At nightfall he had run his single ship in under the land to a small seaport held by the Saracens, who were then celebrating one of their great festivals, and, in the arrogant confidence of long success, had not even closed their gates at sunset. Taking advantage of this, Harold and his men burst into the town—fifty against a thousand—fired the place over their heads, and hastily freeing and arming the Christian slaves, routed and all but destroyed twenty times their number of foes.

A second town, farther up the coast, was taken in a less dashing but more ingenious way. Learning that a fair was about to be held there, Harold borrowed carts and clothes from the native peasants, who lent them with right good will on hearing how they were to be used, and sent forward some of his men disguised as marketers. These, once in, promptly attacked and overpowered the gate guards, and let in the rest of the Norsemen, who were masters of the town ere their astounded foes could understand what had happened.

The fame of these exploits flew abroad like wildfire, and men came flocking from every side to join the great captain; for the spirit was already astir which, half a century later, was to hurl all Europe on Asia in the First Crusade. The patriot who fought to save his country from oppression, the penitent who fought for pardon, the rover who fought for booty, the wild warrior who fought for mere fighting's sake, alike crowded round the raven banner, till Harold's one warship had grown to a fleet, and his single crew to an army.

Alarmed at the rapid success and ever-growing strength of this new foe, the Moslems gathered all their fighting men to crush him at once, and marched against him with a force double his own.

Between the two armies ran a deep and rapid river, over which Hardrada sent a part of his men, whom the Saracens hastened to attack at this seeming disadvantage, fully expecting to destroy them ere the rest could come up. But just as the fight was at the hottest, the wary Harold, who had passed the river by night at another point, fell suddenly on their rear with his main body; and thus assailed on both sides at once, the enslavers of Sicily were crushingly defeated.

In all these frays Kenneth and Fillan had played their part manfully, holding this rescue of their fellow-Christians from the cruelties of brutal and ferocious tyrants to be a just and holy work, as it certainly was when not stained, as too often happened, with cruelty matching that of the Saracens.

But just as Hardrada seemed in a fair way to conquer Sicily, one of the sudden, boyish longings for a new scene of action, which so often perplex one in the history of these grown-up children, hurried him off to the coast of North Africa, where, for several months together, he swept all before him in one unbroken career of victory—storming Moslem fortresses; routing armies thrice as strong as his own; sacking ancient palaces, which he and his men believed to be the work of spirits; slaying, like another David, Saracen Goliaths in single fight; and, like our own Admiral Blake on the same coast six centuries later, freeing Christian slaves by the hundred and burning pirate ships by the score.

But while he was absent, the cowed Arabs in Sicily, emboldened by a false report of his death, plucked up heart again; took arms against the Christians once more, and even gained a few slight successes, which, magnified as usual by rumour, half undid the effect of their late disasters. Day by day the fierce Saracens grew stronger and bolder; and all was going ill for the Christian cause when, just in time, back came Hardrada and his men.

The great captain did not take long to learn how matters stood, and to see that the Saracens' chief strength lay in the fortified town of Ponterotto, whence they were constantly sallying to raid the surrounding country, and in which they stored up, on their return, the booty they had taken.

Not a word said Prince Harold when he heard all this; but he "looked full grim," as old Saemund expressly said, and two days later he was besieging Ponterotto with five thousand men at his back. But this time it really seemed as if for once he had taken in hand an enterprise too hard even for him.

The town was too strong to be taken by storm, and battering engines he had none. The Saracens within, soldiers and townsmen together, outnumbered the whole besieging army. The defenders were expecting help from without in no long time; and confident of being able to hold the town till then, they mocked from their walls at the "bird-catching" in which the besiegers were so strangely engaged.

But they might well be at a loss to understand this strange occupation, for the very men who spread the nets understood it as little as they.

When Hardrada the day before had bidden his men catch as many small birds as they could, they were naturally surprised at such an order, and made merry over it among themselves, with that blunt humour with which the free Norseman was wont to speak his mind to kaiser and king; but no one dreamed of objecting, for, apart from the general conviction that their leader was one who must be obeyed, his own followers believed in him as firmly as men could do, and even his foreign recruits had already learned that, as his quaint old northern biographer has said, "Harold was such a one that, whatever course he took in time of need, all men might afterwards see it was the best."

So the nets were spread and the birds caught as commanded.

It was the seventh night of the siege—a gloomy, dismal, stormy night, without moon or star, and black as pitch. But the Saracens on the walls were surprised, and somewhat dismayed, to see all at once a great number of pale spots of light, very much like a swarm of gigantic fireflies, shooting up through the blackness from the hostile camp, and winging their way to the town.

"What means this?" faltered a startled sentinel. "Hath the northern wizard's magic raised against us a swarm of evil spirits?"

To any man of that age such an idea was not only possible but quite natural; and brave as they were, the stout Moslems shuddered, one and all.

"See, see!" cried a second man, "one of the demons hath perched on the thatch of yon roof; and look! the roof is beginning to burn. Fire! fire!"

"Fire! fire!" echoed half a dozen voices in chorus, as flames broke out in every part of the town at once as if by magic.

Hardrada's fatal stratagem had succeeded but too well, and the bird-catching at which the doomed defenders had jested proved fearful earnest for them.

The birds thus caught, whose nests were in the dry thatch of the houses, had been let loose, with strips of lighted tow or straw attached to them.

Flying back to their homes, they carried the fire with them, which, fanned by the rising wind, ran from street to street till the whole town was one red and roaring blaze.

The panic-stricken Saracens, repenting their fatal over-confidence too late, would fain have fled; but every gate was beset, and those who had never shown mercy now asked it in vain. By morning all was over, and the victors were hunting eagerly in the smoking ruins for their expected booty.

All at once a ghastly form started up from among the Saracen dead and let fly a shaft at Harold himself, who was but a few paces off. The giant reeled, for the arrow had pierced his right arm.

"Take that, destroyer of my people!" gasped the assailant; "and may a dying man's curse go with it!"

And with a faint laugh of defiance he fell back dead, just as the infuriated Northmen rushed upon him in a body.

"Trouble not yourselves for naught, lads," said Harold disdainfully; "deem ye that I am to be hurt by a flea-bite?"

And coolly forcing the arrow-point right through the quivering flesh, he broke off the barb, drew out the headless shaft, and, the wound once bound-up, thought no more of it—for the time.

A born general as well as a born soldier, Hardrada knew the supreme importance of following up a victory at once; and ere the sun was high, he and his men were in full march on Trapani (the ancient Drepanum), the only Saracen stronghold on that coast.

But the wary Moslems were not to be taken by surprise as he had hoped; and on coming in sight of the town he found the gates barred, the walls manned, and all prepared for a stubborn defence.

But beneath all this show of firmness the defenders were irresolute and dismayed; for the fearful news from Ponterotto, brought by two or three fugitives who had escaped the fell reapers of that great harvest of death, and whose tale of "fire-demons raised against them by magic" lost nothing in the telling, cowed with superstitious awe the stern warriors whom no earthly peril could have shaken.

But even this terror failed to awe their leader, Ishak Khan (Chief Isaac), a veteran soldier, brave as a lion and as fierce and cruel as he was brave.

"Against those who serve God faithfully," cried he, "all the wiles of Eblis [the evil one] avail naught. We shall try which is the stronger—the magic of an infidel or the sword of a true believer!"

But the Arab chief, bold as he was, looked troubled when the sunrise showed him Harold's ships sweeping in to blockade the town by sea; for it was ill supplied with food, and a general rising of the Western Sicilians against their tyrants had just cut off all hope of aid by land.

Long and earnestly did Ishak strain his keen eyes toward Harold's camp, on the watch for any movement there. But all was silence and inaction; and for this there was a very good reason, though one that he could never have guessed.

On the previous night, Hardrada, with that boyish joviality that impelled the Norseman of that age to make a holiday of everything, even war, had given a feast in his own tent to a few of his special friends, including, of course, Kenneth and Fillan, as well as old Saemund, Sweyn (Eric's son), Biorn Hare-foot, and Nine-man-Mord.

Hardly had the revel begun when Kenneth became aware of something new and disquieting in the appearance of his friend Harold. The young sea-king's bright, clear eyes looked dull and glassy; his deep, mellow voice had grown strangely hoarse and discordant; and the ruddy freshness of complexion for which he was noted had darkened into a deep flush of unwholesome purple.

But just then our hero's attention was diverted for the moment by Nine-man-Mord, who, accompanying himself on the harp that never quitted him in all his wanderings, broke into an impromptu war-song in honour of Harold's late victory with a burst of savage exultation, of which the two last verses may suffice as a sample :—

"The red tongue of Logi [fire]
　　Hath licked up their town ;
Like leaves of the autumn
　　Their corpses lie strown.

"The ravens cry, 'Brothers !
　　Make haste to your cheer ;
Well fed shall we *now* be,
　　For Harold is here !' "

The last notes were still ringing through the air, when Harold rose to his feet, and filling to the brim the golden goblet that he held, turned to hand it to Mord with a hearty compliment on his song.

But the words that he would have spoken died on his tongue. The ominous flush on his face deepened, a hoarse gasp broke from his quivering lips as the great goblet slipped from his failing hold and clanged on the ground, and ere a hand could be stretched to support him his mighty form sank to the earth like a falling pine !

"The arrow, the arrow !" gasped young Macduff; "it must have been poisoned !"

CHAPTER XX.

DOOMED.

OLD Saemund, the only one of the guests who heard our hero's words, at once clapped his broad hand on the latter's mouth to silence him.

"Hush, lad!" whispered he warningly; "it may be as thou say'st, but 'fewest words, fewest hurts.' Sweyn," added he aloud, "thou hast the most skill of us all in leech-craft; do thou look to him, and we will be gone."

"And hark ye, comrades, not a word of this to any one!" said Sweyn, with grave emphasis and meaning look. "Ye know as well as I that, were it once known that aught is amiss with our Harold, the whole host would melt like snow in spring; so keep your mouths bolted and barred, lads, till we see how the matter goes."

There was little sleep for Kenneth and Fillan that night, and dawn found them both waiting anxiously before Hardrada's tent. But, early as they were, they found Saemund, Biorn Hare-foot, and Nine-man-Mord there before them.

Just then Sweyn, Eric's son, glided noiselessly out of the tent, with a very grave look on his weather-beaten face.

"He liveth yet, thank God!" said the old man in a low voice, reading in their eyes the unspoken question that no one dared to ask; "but he lieth ever unconscious, and as one spellbound, neither moving nor speaking."

Hare-foot and Mord looked gloomier than ever, and young Macduff said vehemently, though still in a cautiously subdued tone,—

"He must not die! he shall not die!"

"That is for God to decide, lad, not for us," said Saemund gravely; "but methinks, since he hath not been sped [killed] at once, there is yet a hope that he will live, for I have ever heard that the poison of the Saracen shafts hath a quick working, even as the venom of their own serpents."

"And it may be," put in Mord, somewhat more hopefully, "that we are, after all, disquieting ourselves in vain. Perchance yon shaft had no poison, and our Harold's ailment may be but the fever of southern lands, for men say these climes are ever unkind to them of the north."

"God grant it be so, lad," said Sweyn fervently, "for then were his hope better. But be that as it may, we must now look to it to keep our men busy, for if they be left idle, ere long they will miss Harold, Sigurd's son, and marvel what hath befallen him."

"Well bethought, comrade," said Saemund approvingly; "it shall be seen to forthwith. Jarl Kenneth, and thou, Jarl Fillan, hie ye quickly to the men of Sicily, who lie yonder along the shore, and give command to them in Harold, Sigurd's son's, name that they cease not to shoot flame-tipped arrows into the town, if haply they may fire the thatch of the houses, as at Ponterotto.——Biorn, haste thee to the quarters of the Italians from Calabria, and lead them forth to scour the country for cattle, sheep, and goats; if there be any within a day's march, I trow *they* will find them, for they are born thieves every man.——Mord, go thou to where the Danes are posted, on the far side of the camp, and bid them go see if there be any way to board the Saracen ships in the inner harbour, or to cast down rocks on them where they lie. I myself will have a care of the Northmen that be in our part of the camp."

The old warrior's shrewd and well-planned directions were at once obeyed, with the best possible results. True, the Calabrian foragers brought in but little live stock, and the pirate ships proved to be beyond the reach of attack; while, though the flame-tipped arrows of the Sicilians set the houses on fire again and again, the flames were speedily quenched by the prompt energy of the defenders. But none the less did the wary old Norseman fully attain his object, which was not so much to make any serious assault on the besieged, as to find constant and engrossing employment for the besiegers.

In fact, during that whole day and the next, the latter were too fully occupied with their various tasks to notice that their leader was no longer among them, but to the few who were in the secret those two days were one long torture.

Not only were they racked with ceaseless anxiety as to the fate of the man whom they loved more than their lives, but they were also haunted by the hardly less intolerable thought of being put to shame before the " unbelieving dogs " by the collapse of the siege, which, if Harold died, must certainly follow the inevitable discovery of his death.

There was not one of these sturdy champions who would not rather have died on the battlefield than have lived to endure such a disgrace, and brave old Saemund only spoke the thoughts of all his comrades when he said, in a growl like a rising thunderstorm, that during that time of trial "every hour seemed as long as a year."

But a harder trial than even this was yet in store for them.

When the third day came the anxious twelve saw but too clearly that if their men did not actually guess the truth, their suspicions were so far aroused by Hardrada's prolonged absence, that any moment might bring the fatal discovery which would ruin all, and old Saemund, in his utter desperation, took a sudden and startling resolution.

That afternoon the Saracens, while watching from their ramparts every movement in the hostile camp, heard a trumpet sound a parley, and saw an Italian soldier, with a white sash tied to his spear by way of a flag of truce, come forward and ask to speak with the Moslem commander.

Prompt at the word, above the parapet rose the tall sinewy form and dark stern face of Ishak Khan.

" What wouldst thou with me, Christian ? " asked he grimly.

" Thus saith our chief," replied the soldier in the "Lingua Franca" of the Mediterranean, that curious mixture of Italian and Arabic which formed the usual

means of communication between the two races.
" Take warning and yield, ere it be too late. If we
take the town, ye die every man of you, and take it
we must, for the Christian cause hath triumphed
through all Western Sicily, and many thousands are
coming to our aid. Give up the town to us peaceably, and all who are not warriors shall be free to
abide in their homes unharmed, and they of the
garrison shall go forth with their ships, having first
sworn by the tomb of your prophet never to set foot
in Sicily again."

The Arab laughed—a short, hard, cruel laugh.

" If these be the words of your chief," said he,
with an ominous grin on his lean, wolfish face, " why
does he not speak them himself? Is the Son of
Hardness dead, or sick? or what is he doing, that I
see him not?"

At these last words old Saemund, who was standing within ear-shot, felt his blood run cold.

Had the foe, then, an inkling of the fatal truth?
If so, all was lost.

But though his heart was heavy as lead, the old
man said as boldly as ever,—

" Our chief lives, and what he is doing you will ere
long learn to your cost."

He threw into his tone all the menacing significance that he could, as he stepped forward to confront the Arab leader, who had turned away for a moment to give some order to his men, and as the Khan faced round again, Saemund added pointedly,—

"In the meantime, I command here in his stead, and I would ask one question—how long will thy store of food hold out?"

It was a chance shot, but it went straight to the mark.

With all his wonderful self-command, Ishak's firm face changed slightly as the fatal query was spoken, and that change, faint and momentary as it was, told the shrewd Norseman all he wished to know.

By this time the parley had begun to draw the attention of the besiegers, and up came several of their chiefs, among whom were Hare-foot, Mord, and the two Scots. Just as they did so, the Arab leader, regaining his composure as suddenly as he had lost it, turned again to Saemund, and replied, with a deeper and deadlier emphasis in his clear, stern tones,—

"Christian, hear the words of Ishak Khan. Thou hast told me thy terms, I will now tell thee mine. If by to-morrow's sunrise ye give not up the siege and go hence, leaving us in peace, every one of the Christian dogs now in my hands shall die; and to show ye that I jest not, this fellow here, whom I take to be a priest of your false law, shall be impaled on these ramparts at daybreak before your eyes!"

As he spoke, two savage-looking Moors dragged forward, in full view of the Christian host, a white-haired monk, in whom Kenneth and Fillan, with a thrill of unspeakable horror, recognized their former friend and benefactor, Father Ailred!

"Say ye I am dead? Ye shall see," he roared.

CHAPTER XXI.

WALKING IN DARKNESS.

AMID the dead hush of dumb horror that followed this awful revelation, which froze all the spectators alike, for Fillan's startled exclamation had told them who this helpless captive was, the doomed man's voice was heard, clear and unfaltering as ever,—

"Children, I charge ye, in the name of Heaven, yield nothing to these godless men for my sake. Their torments can but kill the body, and God will give me strength to die for Him."

The listeners' indrawn breath sounded like a hiss amid that tomb-like silence, and even the iron face of Ishak himself, who had been in England and understood the monk's Saxon speech, softened for a moment into a look of honest, manly admiration.

"Truly God hath put much valour into the hearts of these infidels," muttered he; "when my own end comes may I meet it as bravely."

But just then the fearful interest of this strange scene received a sudden and very startling addition.

Cries of wonder and alarm were all at once heard from behind, and through the ever-growing crowd of excited lookers-on came marching, with measured tread, four giant Norsemen, bearing on a litter formed of crossed spears the mighty form of Harold wrapped in a bearskin cloak.

The superstitious Arabs eyed this strange apparition with visible dismay, and it was with a somewhat forced laugh that Ishak Khan called out,—

" Ha, ha! the wizard chief is dead then, and these fathers of asses think to terrify us with the sight of his corpse ! "

Hardly had he spoken, when Hardrada, to whom a whisper from Mord, in reply to his hasty question, had just told what was going on, started half-erect on his rude couch, tossing aside the bearskin mantle and revealing in all its grand proportions a frame worthy of Hercules himself.

" Say ye I am dead ?   Ye shall see ! " he roared in a voice so mighty that, coming from one who but a moment before had seemed at his last gasp, it terrified the superstitious Moors with the conviction that their dreaded foe had actually risen from the grave to complete his vengeance. "Hearken, dogs! if harm be done by you to this good man, or to any other of your captives, I vow on the faith of a Christian that for every hair of his head I will take the life of an unbeliever!"

"My son," said Ailred rebukingly, "is it thus that a Christian should speak?"

But upon that terrible burst of wrath the gentle rebuke fell as vainly as a dewdrop on a raging furnace.

"For every Christian ye have in your hands," went on Harold fiercely, "we have ten infidels in ours, and on the morrow they shall die, every cur of them, if ye give not up to us this good monk and all the rest. When we take the town we will burn in it every living thing that is therein, *as I am a Christian man;* and as for thee, snarling wolf," he added, darting a flaming glance at Ishak, "we will so deal with thee that thou shalt pray for death long ere it comes."

The listening Arabs looked more and more dismayed, but the grim Khan, chilled for a moment by the freezing touch of superstition, was his own daring self again at the first sound of a threat, and signing to his guards to take away the monk, he replied as boldly as ever,—

"When the morrow's sun riseth, father of big words, thou shalt see how much I care for thee and thy threats. When my head is in thy hands thou may'st work thy will, but thy heart is now in mine."

As the Moor vanished after this defiance, Harold sprang to his feet as if nothing were amiss with him and to the amazement of all who saw it, strode away at a rapid pace toward his own tent.

"Wert thou distraught, man," said Biorn Hare-foot to one of Hardrada's four bearers, who were staring blankly after their vanishing chief, "to let him come forth in such a plight, when it might well have cost him his life?"

"He would not be controlled," said the other, with a meaning shrug of his shoulders; "and not for all the treasures of Mickle-gard [Constantinople] would I gainsay *him* in his mood."

"Thou hast done wisely, lad," said old Sweyn, who, having fallen asleep from sheer weariness, had awoke to find his patient gone, and at once hurried in quest of him. "I wot well that when he is at such a pass it would harm him more to gainsay him than to give him his will, and I am sore mistaken if, ere long, ye see him not whole and sound as ever."

And, to the amazement of the whole army, the old man proved to be right.

Whether Harold's iron constitution had triumphed over the effects of the poison; whether there was no poison to triumph over, and his ailment was only due to the unwholesome climate; or whether, as often happens in such cases, the shock that he had just undergone was the kill-or-cure turning-point of his sickness—the great sea-king was so far himself again by nightfall as to take food for the first time since his collapse, and to receive a few of his friends, among whom he naturally expected to see Fillan and young Macduff.

But when he asked for them they were nowhere to be found, and sorely amazed would he have been could he have seen where they were at that moment, and how they were employed.

The two brave lads had rushed wildly away, frenzied by the seemingly hopeless peril of the man to whom both owed so much. To remain still for a moment beneath the goad of that haunting thought was simply impossible, and with the restlessness of all strong natures under affliction, they hurried off toward the sea, with a vague idea of doing something, no matter what, to save the doomed victim.

" Ere he shall die," cried Fillan vehemently, " we will tear down the wall with our bare hands ! "

" Perchance," said Kenneth, practical even in his

deep distress, " we may find, if we search well, some spot where the wall is weak or mouldered away, and then—"

Here his speech was cut short by a sharp crash and a rattle of falling stones, and then Fillan found himself alone, his comrade having vanished as if the earth had swallowed him.

" What hath chanced, lad? art thou hurt?" cried Fillan, peering over the edge of the deep hollow on the brink of which he was standing.

" Hush!" said Macduff from below, in a tone which, though cautiously subdued, was tremulous with excitement. " Come down hither, quick!"

Down scrambled Fillan, and found to his surprise that what he had taken for a dry torrent bed was a half-destroyed passage, paved and faced with hewn stone, and seeming to vanish into the earth just beyond them.

They looked at one another, and each saw his own thought in the other's face.

" Think'st thou it is indeed so?" whispered Fillan.

" I am sure on't," said Kenneth, in the same tone. " It is one of the magic works of the Roman heathen, wrought by Virgilius the Enchanter, belike, or by some other sorcerer of old time. God be praised that we have found such aid in our sorest need. Forward!"

Forward they went without hesitation into the black, tomb-like mouth of the underground tunnel, which had, as they thought, been a Roman sewer.

It was no easy task to force their way in through the mass of briars and wild grass that all but choked it; but once inside, they got on more easily, for though the passage was so low that they had to crawl on their hands and knees, yet just at first their advance was almost unimpeded.

But none the less was it hard and exhausting work. The water that dripped from the roof wet them through and through; they were chilled to the very bone by the deadly damp of that sunless catacomb; and, used as they were to the free breath of heaven, the close, foul, heavy air oppressed their labouring lungs till every breath was a convulsive gasp.

All at once Kenneth felt his way blocked by what seemed a solid mass of masonry.

His heart stood still at the thought that the hope which had dawned so unexpectedly on their gloomiest despair might be vain after all. But to his great relief, the obstacle proved to be but a single block, which had probably sunk in from above, and a mighty effort forced it aside so far as to give them passage.

Just then Fillan uttered a stifled cry, as he felt on his bare wrist the gliding motion of a thing alive and the touch of the cold, clammy skin of a snake.

The thought of such a death in such a place made even the bold Scots shudder, but Ailred's peril steeled their nerves, and on they went unflinching.

Closer and closer grew the air, chiller and chiller waxed the death-damp of that living tomb, and as they plunged deeper and deeper into the eternal night, strange and ghastly fancies began to beset them. What if they found no outlet at the other end? what if, as seemed quite possible to them, the "magic passage" suddenly closed on them and crushed them? what if another block fell behind them and sealed them up for ever in that dismal dungeon, to die in lingering agony?

But all at once came to their ears, dull and faint, a measured tramp overhead, and the brave lads felt their hearts leap at a sound which they instantly understood. A moment later they saw ahead of them a pale gleam of light, and dragging themselves over a heap of rubbish and then writhing through a tangled briar-clump, they came once more into the outer air, in a deep, bush-clad pit within the walls of the besieged town.

"Thank God!" said Fillan, drawing a long breath.

Let us go back now with all speed, and bring in our comrades to the rescue ! "

" In good time art thou come, Bairam, I was well-nigh asleep on my feet."

" Good is thy luck that thou didst it not, friend Selim, for our captain, even Ishak Khan, knoweth not mercy for him who sleeps on his post. But what of the Christian monk ? "

" I trow he sleepeth too, for I have not heard him stir," said Selim, who was on guard at the door of Ailred's prison.

" He sleepeth ! " echoed Bairam in amazement. " Nay, if he can sleep to-night with impalement awaiting him on the morrow, he must in truth be—"

That sentence was never finished. All in a moment the speaker's horror-stricken eyes beheld, as he thought, a man all on fire start up through the earth, and ere he could move or cry out a stroke laid him dead, and the next moment a second blow dispatched his comrade.

Quick as thought, the man with the lamp thrust his light into the nearest thatch, and as it blazed up two more men broke from the underground tunnel, and rushing to the gate, unbarred and threw it open, and in burst a wave of armed men with a mighty shout, Hardrada himself at their head.

Out rushed the Arabs pell-mell, with any arms they could seize ; but surprised, disordered, and hardly knowing yet what had happened, they fell before the charge of their foes like corn before the reaper.   In a trice the whole town was in the besieger's hands, and a large part of it already on fire.

Through this maddening tumult Kenneth and Fillan, who had guided the party that entered by the tunnel, went straight to Father Ailred's dungeon, eager to free him with their own hands.   It was no light task to break the good monk's strong fetters, but they did it at last, and the three sallied out just in time to witness a very startling scene.

A few Saracen veterans had thrown themselves into a strong tower in the heart of the city, which they held so stoutly that their assailants set fire to it as the easiest way to get them out, and just as the fire was at its hottest, forth broke from it headlong— his hair singed, his beard burned away, his clothes actually scorching from his back, but still undaunted as ever—the terrible Ishak Khan himself !

So fierce was his rush that it carried him clear through the ring of shouting foes, and he might have escaped after all had not Harold in person thrown himself across his path. The weapons clashed together for a moment, and then down went the fierce Arab as if crushed by a falling mountain.

" Spare him, my son ! " cried Ailred, springing between conqueror and conquered so suddenly that the sweep of the sea-king's axe all but struck him down.

Harold uttered a cry of dismay and let fall his terrible weapon.

" Dost thou plead for me, old man ? " said the prostrate Moor faintly—" for me, who would have tortured and slain thee ? "

" I do," said the old monk firmly, " in the name of Him whom I serve, and who bade us love our enemies."

The fallen man looked wonderingly up at him for an instant, as if hardly understanding his words, and then he replied feebly,—

" Christian, thou art braver than I, and I ask thy forgiveness.   It is too late to plead for me, for I have gotten my death, but I repent me that I would have wrought thee harm, for I see now that even an unbeliever may have the law of charity in his heart."

Such were the last words of Ishak the Saracen.

" So should all brave men die ! " muttered Harold Hardrada, as he reverently covered with his own cloak the still face of his dead enemy. " I would he had been a Christian, for he would have made a right good one."

" Thou hast done well, my son," said Ailred gently. " Believe me, it is nobler to spare than to slay, and when I meet the Thane Macduff in England, whither I return forthwith, my mission to Rome being ended, I will tell him that his son is serving with a captain who can ' rule his spirit' as well as ' take a city.' "

CHAPTER XXII.

MIDNIGHT TREACHERY.

B RIGHTLY shone the summer sun on the busy
streets of Constantinople, buzzing like a hive
with the ceaseless bustle of twenty-six nations. Its
cloudless glory lightened the grimness of the huge
gray walls that girdled the ancient town, tipped with
gold many a tall pillar and many a stately church
tower, and kindled into living fire the smooth, shining
Bosphorus, framed in the leafy beauty of those sunny
green hills that even now, after four blighting centuries of Turkish misrule, are the admiration of every
traveller ; and high above, the "castles of Europe
and Asia" (since rebuilt by the Turks) frowned at
each other across the glittering strait, like giants
defying each other to the battle.

The rays that lit up the gilded sterns and painted
oars of the countless boats that flitted like fireflies
over the clear, bright waters, were flashed back from
the polished helmets and huge battle-axes of the

stalwart sentinels who stood on guard on the walls
or paced to and fro at the gates of the vast white
palace of Constantine Monomachus, the Greek emperor, who, thus guarded, little dreamed of the day
when Moslem conquerors should trample his empire
in the dust, and the last Byzantine ruler perish in
vain amid the ruins of his lost capital.

At these men the passing Greeks glanced stealthily,
with the same mingling of wonder, dislike, and
terrified admiration with which their descendants
were one day to eye the dreaded "Janissaries" of
the Turkish Sultan.

Nor was this without reason; for these giant
sentries belonged to the emperor's famous "Varanger
Guard," recruited and officered, as their light hair and
fair faces showed, from the very Northmen who were
then the terror of the Mediterranean, and reverencing
no authority but that of the emperor himself. They
had long been a name of fear to the unwarlike
Greeks, though, to do them justice, they were equally
formidable to the fierce Scythians and Moslems who
unceasingly assailed the tottering empire.

All at once two men were seen coming down the
hill from the great church of Santa Sophia, at whom
the natives looked with less aversion, though they
too plainly belonged to the dreaded life-guard.

Their gold chains and ornamental dress and arms told that both were officers in the household brigade; otherwise their equipment was the same as that of the private soldiers on duty before the palace.

Both carried the huge double-bladed axe always used by the guard, and wore the gilt dragon-crested helmet and light silver cuirass that formed the "undress uniform" of the Varangers worn by them in the capital in time of peace, their heavier armour being reserved for the battlefield. A close-fitting purple frock (the imperial colour) came down to the knee, leaving the lower limbs bare save for the crossing and recrossing of the thongs that made fast their sandals; and each man had at his left side a short curved sword of Eastern make, in a sheath of ivory studded with gold.

But the most curious part of their uniform was a shaggy cloak hanging from the shoulders, seemingly made of bearskin, but really a skilful imitation of it in strong, thick silk, so admirably contrived as to deceive at a little distance the keenest observer.

"Good cause have we, comrade Kenneth, to remember this day with thanks and offerings," said the shorter of the two, with a backward glance at the church they had just left. "In truth, it has been the beginning of great things for us."

" Ay, truly, Fillan lad. Little dreamed we of all that was to come of it when Harold freed us from the clutches of yon Moorish rogues, this day seven years agone."

It was indeed our heroes who spoke, but their nearest kinsmen would hardly have known the slim, light-hearted, careless boys in these strong, stately, grave-faced men, for though but five years had passed since they took leave of Father Ailred on the shore of Sicily, those five years had done the work of ten. Not only had their boyish frames broadened and heightened into the solid strength of manhood, the lapse of time had changed their faces even more than their figures. Bold and firm as ever, those faces had lost the reckless gaiety of youth, to gain in its place the prudence and self-command of riper years. In a word, the thoughtless, impulsive boys had grown into grave, wise, thoughtful men.

And well might it be so, for into those five years of roving the bold Scots had compressed a whole lifetime, and were fully qualified to enter the far-famed guard, whose title of Varangers, or Varen-gangers, was usually interpreted to mean " Far-goers," or wanderers.

After completing the overthrow of the Saracen tyranny in Sicily, one of the most gallant feats of that age of great exploits, Harold and his comrades, still heading east, had gone from Sicily to Africa, and from Africa to the Holy Land, gathering like rolling snow at every step, as they freed and armed band after band of Christian slaves. Many a daring Moorish corsair rued the day when he first saw the raven flag of the great sea-king, who, anticipating by centuries the feats of Admiral Blake and Lord Exmouth, swept the whole African coast, burning the pirate ships wherever he met them, and freeing hundreds of Christian captives from a bondage worse than death.

Then Hardrada, in sheer boyish love of a hazardous adventure—for there was a good deal of the English schoolboy about these mighty men of old—landed in Palestine, and set out to march right across it with his men to Jerusalem, where it was certain death for any Christian to be seen.

"Beware of the Saracens!" said a Syrian trader who acted as his guide.

"Let them beware of me!" replied the sea-king, with stern significance.

The event proved him right. A two days' march brought him to Jerusalem with his men, unopposed by the startled inhabitants; he knelt and prayed at the Holy Sepulchre, as, half a century later, the heroes of the First Crusade were to kneel and pray there after their last and greatest victory ; he left his gold armlets on the altar as an offering, and then coolly marched back to his ships unmolested by the Saracens, who, during the whole of this wonderful march, were growling round him on every side, without daring to come on.

The fame of this exploit flew before him to Constantinople ; and when he and his men, eager to behold all the rumoured wonders of " Mickle-gard," came sailing into its noble harbour, they were heartily welcomed by the emperor himself, who, pressed as he was on all sides by fierce and unresting foes, lost no time in making to these invincible champions the most tempting offers of pay and plunder, if they would be his soldiers and fight his battles.

To Hardrada himself the idea of new foes to fight and new perils to brave was as pleasing as that of defending their fellow-Christians from insult and wrong was to Kenneth and Fillan ; and the bulk of Harold's rough followers cared little whom they served or with whom they fought, so long as they had their fill of " adventures," always the first thing with these wild men. They promptly agreed to be " the kaiser's men " and enter his service, in which they still remained.

"Kenneth lad," said Fillan, after a brief silence, "I am well a-weary of this service; it is like the perfumed air of the kaiser's hall—no true man can breathe freely in it. Rememberest thou not how, in the old romaunts, it befalleth to a champion to be bound with magic threads, light as gossamer, yet strong as steel? Even so feel I, as one in a spider's web!"

"Of a truth, lad, thou hast said the very words that have been on *my* tongue's end this many a day. Well saith the old rede, 'The Greek wines steal all heads, the Greek women steal all hearts, and the Greek men steal everything.' Rogues in the grain are they all, every one; and if our brother Harold be of my mind, we shall soon look our last on Mickle-gard."

"Of thy mind he will surely be, for he loveth these Greek knaves not a whit more than we do, nor they him. 'Tis a shame for us Varangers even to seem to be commanded by such a fellow as this 'akolouthos' [follower] whom they call our captain, forsooth! Men say he is named follower for that it is his duty to follow the kaiser everywhere; but meseems it is a fit name for one who hath ever a mind to follow rather than to lead, when there is aught of danger in the wind."

The disdainful laugh with which he ended was heartily echoed by Macduff.

"Thou art right, lad ; and even such another as he is yon haughty fellow the proto-spathaire [commander-in-chief] who leads, forsooth, all the kaiser's armies ! Were they to wait till he leads them into battle I trow they might wait long enow ! Howbeit, I misdoubt me he would play us some scurvy trick if he dared, for though an adder be timorous, and cower quickly out of sight, it can sting when the chance offers. But haste thee, comrade, lest we come late to the parade ; I hear the trumpet."

In fact, that afternoon had been fixed for a review of the emperor's best troops in the great square then called the Place of Theodosius (now the Et-Meidaun), to be followed by an open-air banquet on the square itself to all who had taken part in the day's work.

When the Scots reached the ground, between two solid walls of jostling shoulders and heated faces, they saw at once that something was wrong.

The Varangers, in place of keeping their ranks as usual, were heaving like a troubled sea ; the gaily-dressed Greek soldiers facing them seemed equally agitated ; and between the two lines stood the very man of whom they had just been speaking, Gergyros the proto-spathaire, in a blaze of steel and gold, confronting Hardrada himself.

As our heroes came up, they heard Gergyros say in a bullying tone,—

"I tell thee again I claim this post for my Band of Immortals. Give place quickly ; it is I who command it ! "

The sea-king's handsome face glowed like heated iron, but his deep voice was perfectly and almost ominously calm as he replied,—

" It is thy master, the emperor, who commands that we Varangers hold the post of honour on the right of the line ; and till he shall order otherwise, here will we bide. Well named are thine ' Immortals,' since they, like thyself, so heedfully avoid all risk of death ; but I have yet to learn that their deeds in war have earned them the right to rank before the Varanger Guard."

This biting retort drew a loud laugh from the Varangers, echoed by not a few of the Greeks themselves, with whom the bullying general was no favourite.

" St. Andrew ! " growled Fillan, " dares this Greek hound bid us be gone from our place, like stray dogs ? Now, if he but presume to—"

" Let be, comrade," said Kenneth quietly ; " I trow Harold is well able to care for that matter himself."

In fact, just as Gergyros was repeating his arrogant demand more insolently than before, the Norse giant suddenly clutched him by both arms and lifted him clear off his feet like an infant, though the weight of his armour was no trifle, saying sternly,—

"Fair words, my mannikin, if thou wouldst not have me fling thee into the Bosphorus like the carcass of a street dog. Wert thou not the kaiser's servant I would do it forthwith; but beware of ever again speaking thus to Harold, Sigurd's son, of Norway!"

And giving him a slight shake, such as a nurse might give to a peevish child, Hardrada set the crestfallen general down again.

After this all went smoothly, and the review was a great success; but as it ended, Macduff whispered to Harold in passing,—

"Brother Harold, take heed what thou eat'st and drink'st at the banquet to-night, for, as I said to Fillan but now, an adder may be timorous, but it can sting."

Long and jovial was the revel, and as it neared its close a richly-dressed attendant came up to Hardrada with a brimming goblet of gold, and said with a low obeisance,—

"The illustrious lord proto-spathaire prays the

bravest of the Varanger champions to drain this bowl to the health of his most sacred majesty the Emperor of the Romans."

Just then the sea-king felt his foot pressed warningly by that of his neighbour Kenneth, but without the slightest change of countenance Harold rose to his feet, and said loud enough to be heard by all,—

"I drink to the health and prosperity of the most sacred emperor; and may my kind entertainer, the illustrious proto-spathaire, be speedily rewarded as he deserves!"

A gruff chuckle from the Northmen told that they fully understood the double meaning of this apparent compliment with which Harold raised the goblet to his lips. But somehow or other he handled it so awkwardly that just as it all but touched them it slipped from his hold and fell clanging on the ground, every drop of its contents vanishing into the thirsty dust!

Kenneth drew a long breath of relief, and for one instant the proto-spathaire's sleek, smooth face was like that of a demon. The next moment he was his own supple, smiling self once more.

"It behoves me to be watchful this night, for when the bowl fails, then comes the dagger," said

Hardrada with a grim smile an hour later as he and the Scots withdrew to the tents pitched for them and their men in the great square, where they were to remain till the emperor himself came next morning to distribute honours and rewards among them.

"And we will watch likewise, brother Harold," said Kenneth, who shared with Fillan the next tent to Hardrada's; "and if it be as thou say'st, woe to any Greek hound who dares come hither on such an errand!"

But though the wary Scots kept watch by turns during the whole night they neither saw nor heard anything suspicious.

It was already almost daybreak, and Kenneth, whose turn it was to watch, was beginning to think that the courage of the would-be assassins must have failed them when he heard, or thought he heard, a stealthy step.

Then something brushed past his tent-door, and then came the dull thud of a heavy blow from the tent of Harold Hardrada.

Macduff sprang to the spot like a tiger, shouting with all his might, but just then Harold's tent fell with a crash, knocking down and burying Kenneth in its fall.

CHAPTER XXIII.

THE SECRETS OF A PALACE.

"WHAT means all this uproar in the city?" asked a bare-limbed peasant, who, driving his laden donkey before him, had just come up to one of the landward gates of Constantinople, which had been opened at dawn as usual.

"These Varanger demons are up in arms, and have dared to beset the palace of the most sacred emperor himself," said the soldier to whom he spoke, who did not look very soldier-like just then, for he was white as a sheet and trembling like a leaf. "They demand redress, men say, for some wrong done to their leader; and if the barbarians once break loose, may the saints help us all, for no man's life will be safe."

The worthy warder's panic was general in the city on that eventful day, and certainly not without reason.

Just after sunrise the sentries on the palace walls had been startled by such a clamour as they had seldom heard, and beheld a wave of shining helmets, and furious faces, and tossing arms, and glittering weapons come rushing and roaring over the open space before the great gate, while shouts of "Treason!" "Justice!" "The emperor!" "Vengeance!" made the air ring.

Some of the Greek soldiers would have resisted, for a few brave men were still to be found even amid the effeminate subjects of this rotting empire. But the rest implored them for pity's sake to speak peaceably to "these wild beasts of the north," who would otherwise murder them all; so an officer of rank looked over the wall, and cried with a forced show of friendly confidence,—

"How now, good friends? What seek ye here? This is no guise in which to come before the palace of his most sacred majesty the emperor!"

"We free Northmen," replied old Saemund grimly, "come where we will, and in what guise we like. Our leader's life hath been attempted by treachery, and we will have the traitor dealt with as he deserves. Let the emperor do us justice speedily, or we will do it for ourselves."

Just then the "follower" (nominally captain of the Varangers) appeared on the wall to address the raging throng. But though popular with these wild warriors from his liberality and the goodwill he had always shown them, he had no sooner begun to speak than his voice was drowned by a din to which all the former uproar was nothing.

"Prate not to us!" roared Nine-man-Mord; "this matter is for thy master's handling, not for thine. Go tell the emperor we must speak with him face to face; and haste thee, for high as thou standest, methinks a well-flung dart may reach thee even up there."

The hint was not lost on the worthy follower, who vanished as if the earth had swallowed him, and a few minutes later rose slowly above the parapet, with visible reluctance, the flowing robes and pale, weak, peevish face of the Emperor Constantine Monomachus.

"If ye ask justice, my valiant Varangers, justice ye shall have—my ears are ever open to such an appeal," said he graciously, though the voice that he tried to make firm and impressive faltered into a tremulous whine. "But where is your leader who hath had the wrong? Let him stand forth and tell his case boldly."

A second shout, which seemed to shake the very earth, broke forth as Hardrada's golden helmet was seen towering far above the tallest crests of that chosen band as he came striding through them.

"Hearken, kaiser," cried the young Goliath, eyeing the cowering emperor as a lion might eye a jackal, "and pardon me if I speak brief and blunt, as is the wont of us free Northmen. Yester-eve thy servant the proto-spathaire would have ousted us from the place appointed us by thee at all public parades, and forasmuch as he would not yield when I gainsaid him, I was constrained to speak unto him somewhat plainly in the hearing of all, which doubtless vexed him; wherefore he would have poisoned me at the banquet, and that failing, sent one of his men to stab me in my sleep."

A growl like a rising storm billowed through the Varanger ranks, and the poor emperor quaked to the tips of his imperial shoes.

"Have ye caught the assassin?" asked he tremulously.

"My men slew him," said Harold carelessly, as if such a trifle were hardly worth mentioning; "but there were some who knew him for one Stephanos Epimenes, a soldier of the 'Immortals;' and thou may'st judge if they spake truth by the fashion of his dagger, which I found sticking in a block of wood that I had laid in my place, with my mantle cast over it."

He held up a long Greek dagger, the eagle-shaped hilt of which was at once recognized by all as the badge of the "Immortal Band."

"Now mark me, Kaiser Constantine," went on Harold with stern emphasis, silencing with a wave of his hand the roar of fury that burst forth, "had he been worthy of it, I would have made fair proffer to thy proto-spathaire to prove his innocence in loyal single combat with me; but men fight not with felons and midnight stabbers, and he who doth the deeds of a coward should have a coward's due. Wherefore we will that thou cast to us presently from the wall the head of the traitor proto-spathaire, or else——"

The glance that he cast over the sea of fierce faces around, and the mighty roar that answered it, amply completed the sentence.

Constantine's thin cadaverous face grew paler than before. For a moment he held a whispered conference with the follower and two or three other court officials, and then vanished into his palace, the courtiers following.

Then sank over the crowded space in front of it a hush so deep that in the midst of that vast multitude a man with his eyes shut might have thought himself alone. A few minutes of silent and gloomy expectation, and then came whirling over the parapet, to fall with a dull thud at Hardrada's feet, a freshly-severed head, the livid and distorted features of which were at once recognized as those of the powerful and haughty proto-spathaire.

A moment later the meagre form and jewelled purple robe of the feeble old man "before whom all trembled," as his flatterers said, though it was rather he who trembled before all, appeared on the walls once more, and waving his hand to the Varangers, he said with a would-be majestic air,—

"My brave soldiers, ye have seen that the emperor's justice is prompt—"

"Ay, when three thousand Varangers demand that it should be so," muttered Biorn Hare-foot with a grin.

"—and ye shall now see," went on Constantine, "that his gratitude is equally so. Our trusty champion, Prince Harold, shall henceforth he lodged in our own palace, and we bid him to our banquet this night, in token of the esteem in which we hold him. Nay, more, it is our will that he take the place and honours of the false traitor whose villainy hath attempted his life. Ere three days are past, sons of the Northland, ye shall hail him as commander of all our armies and proto-spathaire of the empire!"

A loud cheer broke from the Varangers, each of whom felt himself honoured by this tribute to his chosen hero, but Hardrada, silencing the clamour with a wave of his hand, threw back his head like a lion shaking its mane, and bluntly replied,—

"Kaiser, I thank thee, but it may not be. To thy banquet will I come, for it would ill befit me to scorn such courtesy when offered in good faith, but thine honours and rewards are not for me. I purpose to depart forthwith to my own land, being minded to quit as soon as may be a land where men who call themselves Christians use the arms and the treachery of heathen murderers."

At this blunt and scornful rejection of his offered favours the emperor's face changed visibly, and he whispered again with the officers around him. Then turning once more to Hardrada, he said as smoothly as ever,—

"Valiant Harold, we hope to persuade thee to forego a purpose that would rob us of our best warrior. To-night we expect thee at our banquet."

That morning, as ill-luck would have it, Kenneth and Fillan were called away by special duty to a distant part of the town, and it was all but nightfall ere they got back to the Varanger barracks near the palace.

When they did so, the news that awaited them only deepened, in place of allaying, their ever-growing forebodings of evil.

A third of the Varanger Guard had just been sent off to Scutari, on the other side of the strait, the Greek soldiers quartered there having been brought over to the city to fill their place; another third of the guard had been ordered to a village several leagues away, as if for a movement against the rebellious Bulgarians of the north; and thus but a thousand Varangers were left in the whole town.

The simple Northmen told all this in high glee, vowing that the emperor was wise to send his Varangers where there was a chance of action, leaving the lazy Greeks to lounge about the city, or mount guard at the palace like stuffed figures in a pageant, but the clouded faces of the shrewd Scots showed that they were not of the same opinion.

"This bodes no good to Harold, or to us," whispered Kenneth. "Should it come to blows, what avail a thousand men against a host in these narrow streets, where we may be assailed from windows and house-tops? Harold must not go to this banquet; let us warn him forthwith."

But this was easier said than done, for on inquiry they found that Hardrada had left the barrack to go down to his two ships, which were lying in the great harbour known then, as now, by the name of "The Golden Horn."

Thither hurried our heroes, well pleased at these signs of speedy departure. But quick as they were, they came too late ; Harold had already gone to the emperor's banquet.

"But he bade us expect him back this night, and have all ready for sailing," said Sweyn, Eric's son, as the Scots stood in silent dismay ; "and that will we, though I see not how we are to sail forth, for these Greek knaves have but now closed the harbour-mouth with an iron chain !"

At this new proof of impending treason, his hearers looked gloomier still.

"Tush !" said Nine-man-Mord, as coolly as if only speaking of mending a broken spar. "If the worst come to the worst, we can go ashore and kill the guards, and then undo the chain ourselves."

The Scots, not staying to hear him out, were already half-way up the hill to the postern gate of the palace, where they gave the password, and asked to speak with Hardrada. But, as they feared, the officer on duty replied through the grating, politely but firmly, that Harold was the emperor's guest that night, and not accessible to any one.

Just then, as they stood at a loss what to do, up came a richly-dressed black slave, who, bowing low, said in broken Greek,—

"My lords, I take ye for the men I am sent to seek; are ye not, I pray you, Kennetos and Fillanos, the friends of Prince Harold the Hyperborean?"

"We are," said Macduff. "What wouldst thou with us?"

"My mistress, the Lady Pulcheria Comnena, would speak with ye both."

"Ha!" said Kenneth, whose face brightened visibly, "thou rememberest her, Fillan? she whom Harold rescued from yon Saracen thieves when she was on pilgrimage in Holy Land. I knew not she had returned to the city; but if she aid us, all may go well yet," and he signed to the slave to lead the way.

The African led them round the palace to a large and imposing mansion at the back of it, through which they followed him up a winding-stair and along a shadowy corridor, ending in a small cabinet lighted by a hanging lamp of solid silver. Here sat a lady no longer young, but with the stately bearing and noble features which seemed the birth-right of the renowned family that, one generation later, wore the imperial crown of Constantinople.

" Leave us, Zerkon," said she to the slave, " and let
none approach till I have spoken with the northern
lords."

Then turning to the wondering Scots, she went
on,—

" It is long since I last saw you or your comrade
Prince Harold, but I have not forgotten his good
deed, and therefore sent I for you, to tell ye that
he is now in sore peril, and that ye alone can save
him."

" Show us how ! " cried both men with one voice.

" Know, then, that I have learned——ask not how
——that this night at the banquet the emperor will
once more try to persuade Prince Harold to abide
here as proto-spathaire, since, if he depart, not only
do we lose a matchless champion, but with him will
depart many a good warrior whom our armies can
ill spare.   If Harold refuse, down goes he into the
dungeons beneath the palace ; and then is he lost, for
though the emperor would but hold him captive till
he yield, there be many at court that hate him, and a
helpless man's life is soon taken."

The two listeners breathed short and hard.

" Last night," went on the lady, " stood by me in a
dream one all in light, like unto a saint, and thus he
spake, ' Cast ropes down into the Tower of Silence

and save my brother!' When I heard this day what I have told ye, then understood I the dream; but to cast the ropes I need your aid. Follow me."

She led the way up a narrow stair, higher and ever higher, in total darkness—for by this time night had fairly set in—till all at once, passing through either a door or a long window, they felt the cool night air on their heated faces, and found themselves on what seemed a flat house-top.

"From this roof," said she, "the span of an arch joins the Tower of Silence, and by it ye may creep thither, if ye be steady of head and firm of heart. The tower's sides are open, and this rope will let ye down into it. When ye touch ground, turn to the left, and undo the bolts of the third cell; he will be there. I will await here your coming back with him. Go, and God speed ye!"

As she spoke, the faint and spectral gleam of the rising moon showed in all its terrors the appalling task before them.

Amid the great gulf of blackness from which it started out, the slender rib of stone over which they were to pass looked thin and frail as a spider's thread, and though the gloom still hid the fearful depth below, it was all the more terrifying on that account.

" Do ye waver ? " asked their hostess.

" Not we ! " said Macduff bluntly. " Where is the rope ? "

She gave it, and the Scots tested its strength with several violent tugs.

" We doubt not thy good faith, lady," said Kenneth apologetically, " but the cord that bears Harold Hardrada's weight hath need to be strong."

Then silently commending his soul to God the brave man hung the coil of rope round his neck, and closely followed by Fillan, thrust himself boldly forward into the empty air.

Even they, however, did not venture to walk along the coping of the arch, but, sitting astride of it, hoisted themselves along with their hands, a task in itself from which most men would have shrunk.

Around and below, nothing but empty air, save the tiny breadth of stone that upheld them. In front, black and grim, the vast shadowy mass of the palace, like a threatening monster waiting to devour them ; and on either side hideous faces seemed to glare and grin at the doomed men, in the fitful, ghostly moonlight, from the carved turrets and cornices of the adjoining houses.

But as the moon brightened it suggested other terrors more real than these. Should there be a single watching eye at one of those countless windows they were lost, for it was death to enter the palace unbidden.

Hark! was that a murmur of low voices from the roof that they had just quitted? Had Pulcheria betrayed them after all? And when they looked forward, was it only the play of the moonlight, or their own heated fancy, or did a shadowy form peer forth, weapon in hand, from an opening of the tower in front, all ready to strike?

Never yet, in all their countless perils, had the nerves of the adventurous Scots been so sorely tried. But the danger of the man whom they loved more than life steeled them anew, and on they went unwaveringly.

And now they were half-way over the fearful chasm, and but a few yards from the other side. Kenneth reached it at last, and clutched, with the convulsive grasp of a drowning man, the stone balustrade that guarded the open sides of the tower, an ample proof of what he had suffered in that awful passage, and in a moment more Fillan was at his side.

But as the bold men looked down into the tomb-like blackness within, they shuddered to hear, from that gloomy void, faint groans, broken words of agony, and stifled shrieks, as of one in mortal pain or terror.

"It is like going down into hell!" said Macduff with a shiver, as he knotted one end of his cord to the balustrade, and let fall the other into the black abyss; "but Harold is there, and save him we must!"

At that instant came rolling up to their ears a mighty roar, like the cry of some monstrous beast.

A second roar followed, sharper and fiercer than the last, then came a dull crash, and all was still!

CHAPTER XXIV.

FOR LIFE AND DEATH.

AT the emperor's table that night Harold had been restless as a caged lion. Whether from his own disturbed fancy, or from the heady Greek wine with which he was unceasingly supplied, all around him seemed to wear an unearthly and goblin aspect. The noble statues of white marble on either side of the hall were to him like corpses, whose stony faces in the fitful lamplight writhed into a mocking smile; the rich purple wine looked grimly like blood; the guests, blazing with jewels and gold, seemed wrapped in quivering flames; and the pale, meagre, bloodless emperor himself, enthroned in his rich robes at the head of the board, suggested to the Norseman's heated fancy the ghastly thought of a dead king seated in state, arrayed in the costly trappings that were to be buried with him.

Only by a violent effort did the sea-king resist an impulse to spring from his seat and rush out of the hall, so strong was the haunting idea of being at one of the "witch feasts" of his grim native legends, which might end, for all he knew, in his being turned into a wolf or a frog, or spellbound for ever in the depths of the earth.

In such a mood he naturally turned a deaf ear to the emperor's flatteries, and repelled, like the temptation of an evil spirit, his repeated offer of the dignity of commander-in-chief, with the honours and profits attached to it, till Constantine, seeing that he only irritated his guest instead of persuading him, desisted, and rising, said with studied courtesy,—

"Woe is me that I must lose so stout a champion; but if so it must be, I pray thee, that there be no ill-will betwixt us, drain one loving cup ere we part, and bear away the goblet as my farewell gift."

Harold, unwarned by his late experience of Greek "loving cups," emptied the bowl at a draught; but hardly had he done so, when the hall turned blood-red, the guests seemed to swell into giants, all swam around him, and he lost consciousness.

When he came to himself again he thought he must be dreaming. All was pitch dark, and he felt that he was held down by a grasp that fettered alike arms, limbs, and body, as if a dozen iron hands were clutching him at once.

The simple Norseman's first idea was that, as he had feared, he was pent for ever beneath the earth by a magic spell. His next guess was nearer the mark—that the emperor, resolved not to let him go, had stupefied him with some drug, and then immured him in the dungeons whose secrets few had returned to tell.

Furious at such treachery, and reassured by the thought that he had to do with mere earthly forces after all, he put forth his giant strength in an effort that seemed able to rend a solid rock; but the artificer whose infernal skill had wrought the deadly engine in which the Norse Samson was snared had done his work too well, and all Hardrada's struggles were vain.

Bitterly enough, now that it was too late, did the doomed man repent the rash confidence with which he had drained that fatal cup. But just as he was giving himself up for lost, a step was heard outside, followed by the grating of a bolt, and then the door swung slowly open, and a red glare of torchlight showed Harold that he was lying on a rude wooden couch in a rock-cut cell, and that the torch-bearer who had just entered was a gaunt, pale-faced, haggard man, all in black.

Harold naturally took this spectral stranger for

an executioner sent to put him to death, and made
a frantic effort to break loose and grapple with him;
but the unknown laid a finger warningly on his lips,
and whispered,—

"Hush! I am a friend, sent to aid thee; but be
wary, for sharp ears are nigh."

So saying, he touched a spring, and at once the
network of steel rods that fettered Harold vanished
into the wooden frame of the bed so suddenly that
the simple Northman began once more to suspect
witchcraft in the matter.

"Rise and follow!" said his liberator; and he did
not need to be told twice.

Leading him out of the cell, the stranger pointed
to the right, down a gloomy passage, and said in a
lower whisper than before,—

"I dare not tarry, lest we be discovered. Follow
yon passage, and unbar the door at the end; beyond
lies freedom. Farewell! Heaven speed thee!"

Torch and torch-bearer vanished, leaving Hardrada
alone in utter darkness; but with restored freedom
came revived hope and confidence, and there was
even a grim glee in his tone as he said, with a joyful
expansion of his mighty chest,—

"Now that I am free once more, twenty of these
Greek foxes shall not make me captive again!"

He was groping his way down the dark passage, when, stepping on something smooth and slippery, he stumbled and all but fell, and stooping down, he found that he had trodden on a fleshless bone, which felt like that of a man!

It was no pleasant discovery at such a time and in such a spot, especially to one whose own bones might ere long be mouldering in this eternal darkness amid those of the wretches who had perished before him; and brave as he was, he could not repress a shudder when, a moment later, his foot struck another bone, and then another and another!

"Let me once get clear of this den of thieves and murderers," said the brave man, with a thrill of disgust, "and all the kaiser's treasures shall not tempt me back."

As he spoke, his extended hand touched an iron door, which he guessed to be the one spoken of by his guide as having freedom beyond it, and with eager haste he drew back the heavy bar that secured it.

The long, creaking groan with which the door swung back was answered by a terrific roar which awoke every echo of the sunless vaults, and a faint glimmer of light from above showed to Harold, right in front of him, the huge shaggy head, gaping jaws, and fiery eye of a monstrous lion!

Ere he had time to draw back, the monster was upon him. But quick as was the beast, the man was quicker still. He leaped aside, and the lion, missing him, came with a terrific shock against the wall, and uttered a louder, sharper roar of pain and fury. Ere it could make a second spring Harold whirled up the heavy iron bar that he still held, and smote the brute full in the forehead, just where it was undefended by the shaggy mane.

Such a blow was beyond the power of man or beast to sustain, and the stricken monster, with one hoarse gasp, rolled over on its side and lay dead.

"Praise be to God who hath strengthened me!" said the pious Northman; "and could I but scale this tower, which seems open at top, I might yet escape."

Hardly had he spoken, when a well-known voice, the very last he expected to hear in that dismal place, came floating down from above.

"Is that thou, brother Harold?" it asked, in a tone of strong excitement, though cautiously subdued.

"Who speaks to me?" said the startled sea-king.

"I, Kenneth Macduff; and Fillan is with me. Art thou able to climb a rope?"

"That am I, had I but a rope to climb," said Harold cheerily.

"It hangs beside thee. Come quickly up to us, and then is thy way clear."

Hardrada needed no urging. In a trice he was beside his friends, who, having untied and hauled up the rope lest it should betray their kindly hostess, recrossed the perilous arch, and found Pulcheria still on the watch for them.

"Thank God thou art safe, noble Harold," said she ; "but as none must know thou hast been here, I will myself let thee and thy friends out by a secret way ; and bethink thee hereafter that Pulcheria Comnena was not ungrateful."

A few minutes later the three bold men stood alone in the silence of the moonlit street, hardly sure yet that all this was not a wild dream.

But there was no time for musing, and the practical Harold promptly gave the word to move.

"Let us to our ships, and that speedily ! I shall not breathe freely till I am far away from this accursed lair of rogues and liars."

"Have with thee," said Fillan ; "but it befits thee to know that they have closed the harbour-mouth with an iron chain, to stay thy flight."

But Hardrada, making no comment on this startling

news, strode down the hill at a pace that even his active comrades could hardly equal.

As they went, Harold told briefly his late adventures, which the bold Scots heard with burning rage. But whether the pretended friend who had betrayed him to the lion was a partisan of the late protospathaire, or the agent of the offended emperor himself, was never known.

Amid the great mass of shipping that crowded the noble harbour Hardrada's two small vessels were hardly seen, but their captain needed no telling where to find them, and he was warmly welcomed by his expectant crew.

"All is ready, as thou badest, Harold, Sigurd's son," said old Saemund, "and were it not for yon iron chain—"

"Tush!" said the sea-king, "two chains could not bind Fenrir the wolf-demon, and shall one chain bind us? Push we out now into mid-harbour, as if we were but changing our berth; and then, when the night is somewhat older, and all is still, out of this trap will we go, let the Greek curs do what they will."

The men obeyed without a word, sure that their leader would make good his promise, though none knew how. He had said it, and that was enough.

But though outwardly as brave and cheery as ever, the great captain was secretly racked with such anxiety as he had never felt before. At any moment his escape might be discovered; at any moment he might see the spears and helmets of the emperor's men come glittering down the slope to drag him back to his dungeon; and he set his teeth grimly as he vowed that they should never take him alive.

The night wore on. Little by little the lights went out in the great mass of houses above, and all was still, save the senseless laugh of some belated drunkard, or a stifled cry telling of violence and robbery.

"Now!" said Harold at last, and instantly both his ships flew right at the chain that barred their way.

As they neared it the rowers bent to their oars so mightily as almost to lift the light ships out of the water, and the rest, by Hardrada's order, crowded to the stern, each with a chest or bag in his arms.

The weight being thus thrown astern, the prow rose quite clear of the water, and partly from this cause, partly from the tremendous impetus of their rush, both ships ran so far up on to the chain as to be almost balanced on the top of it. Then, at

Harold's word, the men in the stern sprang forward to the bow, burdens and all, thus depressing the *Serpent's* prow till she slid off the chain into the water outside!

But just then a fearful crash told that the *Pike* had been less fortunate. Unable to bear the strain, she had broken her back and sunk with all her stores; but her crew swam stoutly, and were all picked up by their comrades.*

It was high time, for the alarm was already given. Lights were seen glancing to and fro, men were heard calling to each other, and a splash of oars from both sides of the harbour at once told that boats were putting off to learn the cause of the disturbance.

But the discovery came too late. Between the Bosphorus and the coast of Egypt there was no vessel that could match the *Serpent* in speed, and long ere sunrise her daring crew were far beyond pursuit.

* For this escape, see Snorro Sturlason's "Heimskringla."

CHAPTER XXV.

HOME AT LAST.

NIGHT was falling over the north-east coast of England on a gloomy, stormy evening in the autumn of 1055. Far down among the western mountains the last gleam of a red and angry sunset was fading into the huge mass of leaden cloud that had overspread the whole sky; and, beyond the mouth of the Tyne, all was one restless welter of tossing waves, the foamy crests of which looked white and ghastly beneath the deepening dimness of the coming storm.

A strong north-east gale, blowing fiercer and fiercer every moment, was hurling all the might of the North Sea on that perilous coast in roaring hills of foam; and well might the group of men on the tall gray tower that guarded the river mouth—barely able to keep their feet against the furious blast, strong as they were—shake their heads meaningly as they gazed seaward in quest of a passing sail.

True, any ship from that quarter was more likely to be foe than friend; for in that age of Danish invasions and pirate raids the east coast of England was never safe for a single day, and this river fort was then the only building that dared to show itself where now the houses of North Shields and South Shields mass themselves along either bank, and where the Newcastle holiday-makers crowd Tynemouth beach by thousands every summer.

But these bold Saxons and Anglo-Danes, themselves in constant peril, could pity and aid any man in distress, even if they had to fight and slay him but an hour later.

"Heaven help any who have not yet run for the land!" said a tall man in the midst of the group, "though methinks none can be so foolhardy. Yet, unless my eyes deceive me, I espy a sail yonder."

"They deceive thee not, lord earl," said a deep voice at his side: "there *is* a sail there, and lo, even as I speak, another!"

Then all stood silent, watching intently the two storm-tossed ships, which were plainly making for the shelter of the river-mouth.

Most interested of all seemed the man addressed as "earl," who towered high above the tallest of his stalwart companions, and showed a strength that might have worsted many a younger man, though his hair was gray as the moss-grown tower itself, to which his aged but still massive frame might have been fitly compared.

" Methinks the one is of Moorish build, as were she a Saracen trader or corsair," said one of the watchers.

" And I deem the other a Northland rover," cried a second; " for there be shields ranged along her gunwale, and she flieth the raven flag."

" Ha!" said the earl, with a grim smile, " if she come in peace she shall be welcome; and if in war, she shall not lack a right Saxon greeting. Be that as it may, she is a good ship and well handled."

So in truth she was; for though billow after billow broke over her, and the water could be seen streaming from her sides like a cataract as she rose from each plunge, on she came in gallant style, fighting her way in the teeth of all that wind and wave could do.

And now both vessels were within easy reach of the river-mouth, when suddenly a heavy squall of rain burst upon them, blotting them out as if they had never been; and the old warrior shook his gray head gloomily, as if doubting whether he should ever see them again.

But when the squall passed, both ships were safely

entering the river; and the stately earl clapped his hands like a boy, with a lusty shout of glee.

"Well and manfully done!" he cried. "Go down quickly, Edric, and bid the strangers hither as my guests; or hold, I will go myself, for well have they earned whatever courtesy we can do them."

Down he hurried to the beach; and as he reached it, stepped ashore from the nearest ship a form of such giant height as to overtop even his own.

The two giants eyed each other for a moment in silent admiration.

"Thou art a man, be who thou mayst," said the earl heartily. "Men call me the tallest man in Northumbria, yet must I look up to thee. What is thy stature?"

"Five ells of Norway" (eight feet), said the tall stranger.

"There lives but one man of such measure, and I deem thee to be Harold Hardrada. Welcome, noble Harold! seldom comes such a guest to Siward of Northumbria."

"Siward of Northumbria?" echoed a younger and smaller man at Harold's side. "Art thou in truth Earl Siward the Stout? Suffer me, then, to offer my warmest thanks to the kindly host of my banished father."

"Thy banished father, say'st thou? Then thou art Kenneth Macduff. Right glad will thy father be, I trow, to welcome thee home again."

"He liveth yet, then?" said Kenneth, drawing a long breath of relief.

"That doth he, God be praised, in his own hold by the Forth, Earl of Fife once again, and the trustiest servant of King Malcolm Canmore."

And then, as the newcomers followed him up the hill, he told briefly the stirring events of the last few years, of which they knew nothing.

Siward's own entreaties, and those of the exiled Prince Malcolm, had at last overcome the habitual apathy of King Edward the Confessor, and the great earl had been sent north with an army to punish the usurper Macbeth and set Malcolm on his father's throne. Macbeth, fearless and resolute to the last, had turned to bay at Dunsinane, where Siward's nephew and namesake, and his son Asbiorn (Kenneth's old acquaintance), had both fallen, "with all their wounds in front," as the old man proudly said; but Macbeth himself escaped from the lost battle (though Shakespeare has taught the whole world to think otherwise), only to fall at Lhamfannan a few months later.

King Malcolm's first care was to repay the services

of the elder Macduff, who had been foremost in every peril of the short campaign, by restoring his forfeited lands, and adding a large grant of his own; and the reinstated Thane of Fife, now the greatest man in Scotland after the king himself, had taken charge of Fillan's domain of Lochaber till its owner should return.

"Then must thou and I, Fillan, get us home as quick as may be," cried Kenneth; "and if thy lands have been in my father's keeping, I'll warrant thou wilt find them no whit the worse."

"And I," said Harold, "will lend ye, to bear ye home, yon Moorish craft that we took from the Saracens in the Midgard Sea. Gladly would I go with ye, but I must to Norway with all speed, to see if my nephew Magnus, who reigneth there now, will give up the kingdom to me peaceably, or if he be minded to plead against me in the court of the battle-axe. Howe'er it be, ye two must come shortly to visit me in Norway; and it may well be that I shall one day come to England again."

Little dreaming how strangely and terribly those last words were to be fulfilled, the Scots heartily assented; and, two days later, they were sailing merrily to Fife, and Harold was on his way home to Norway.

"Then thou gat'st the news I sent thee from Sicily, father?" said the younger to the elder Macduff, as he and Fillan sat at meat with him in the old castle by the Forth, which looked just the same as ever, though ages seemed to our hero to have passed since he last saw it.

"That did I, and gladder tidings never came to me yet. 'Twas when I was Earl Siward's guest that thy messenger came; and I trow the good earl rejoiced well-nigh as much as I."

"And how hath it fared, I pray, with the good monk Ailred, who was my bode [messenger] to thee?"

"Monk, say'st thou? He hath stepped far higher than a simple monk long ere now. Many a year hath passed since they chose him prior of his monastery in Chester town, and last Yuletide saw him a mitred bishop in Winchester; nay, so high standeth he in King Edward's grace that, by St. Andrew, it were no marvel to see him archbishop too ere long!"

"They could find no better," cried Fillan, "'twixt the four seas of Britain."

Ere long came news that Hardrada had reached Norway in safety, and that his nephew, Magnus the Good—a very fine lad, though somewhat hot and hasty—had given up his first intention of fighting for the crown, and agreed that they should divide the kingdom peaceably.

The ship that brought the news—commanded by Kenneth's old friend Saemund—carried back young Macduff to be a guest at Hardrada's court. Fillan was just then too busy with his duties as the new chief of Lochaber to be able to go with him; but after that, both men visited Harold in Norway regularly every year.

And then for a time all went well.

Earl Macduff, with his son's help, ruled his recovered earldom of Fife wisely and well. Fillan did the same on his own lands of Lochaber. King Malcolm Canmore—who, fierce, ignorant, and passionate as he was, had enough shrewd sense to appreciate the power of culture and knowledge—was meanwhile doing his utmost to introduce into his own barbarous realm, not wholly without success, the higher civilization that he had seen and admired during his exile in Saxon England.

Even the ever-restless Harold Hardrada—now left sole King of Norway by his nephew's death—seemed inclined to be quiet after all his wanderings and battles, and, unlike most other kings of that iron age, to make his own land happy instead of making other lands miserable. His proposed visit to England was still delayed; but in the meantime he had sent to London, by the hands of old Saemund and Sweyn, Eric's son, rich gifts to the new church, just built in Southwark by the pious Edward in honour of Harold's slain brother, St. Olave—a church which, though long since swept from the earth, has left its name, in a corrupted form, to the famous Tooley Street of modern London.

But all this time the sky was slowly darkening with the coming storm that was to shake all Western Europe.

The first sign of evil was the sudden death of the great Earl Godwin, King Edward's father-in-law. He had long been the real master of England, though the weak and do-nothing king loved him not; and his death struck away a mighty pillar from the tottering Saxon power.

Next went Leofric of Chester, the great Earl of Mercia, whose place was but poorly filled by his rash and fiery son Algar, the father of that Queen Aldyth of Wales at whose court our heroes had been guests, and whose infant daughter had been saved from the wolf by Fillan.

After Leofric—snatched by a timely death from the evil to come—followed the grand old Siward of Northumbria; and, as if to make his loss doubly

fatal to England, he was succeeded in his earldom
by the terrible Tostig, son of Godwin, described by
his own father as " greedy to grasp, but powerless
to hold ; able to ruin, but strengthless to save." And
his misrule and violence soon showed that the censure
was not a whit too severe.

And all this while, like a rising thunder-cloud far
away in the south, grew and grew the ever-strengthen-
ing power of a mightier than all, " William, Count
of the Normans," whom history was one day to call
" William the Conqueror." It was rumoured that
he had designs on the crown of England ; and though
the bold Saxons laughed such an idea to scorn, the
bravest of them felt a secret awe of one who had
never met his match either in council or in fight,
and whose craft was even more dreaded than his
might.

Thus stood matters in the autumn of 1063, when
Kenneth and Fillan, coming home from their yearly
visit to Norway, found news awaiting them that
greatly startled both.

Algar of Mercia, ever fierce and turbulent, and
enraged at some fancied slight from the king, had
openly rebelled and joined their old friend, King
Gryffyth of Wales, in a merciless raid on the Saxon
border. Harold, the greatest of Earl Godwin's sons

and the idol of the whole Saxon people, had been sent to end these ever-recurring troubles once for all; and Gryffyth, defeated in battle after battle, had at last been driven to bay in Pen-maen-mawr itself, where, fiercely refusing all Harold's offers of mercy, he had been treacherously murdered by his own men.

His ally Algar had died of a fever; and Algar's sons, Edwin and Morcar, destined to a sad renown and a terrible fate, had become lords of Mercia, and had given refuge there to their sister Aldyth, King Gryffyth's widow, and her young daughter, Fillan's former playmate.

Everything now hurried onward to the great catastrophe.

Harold, Godwin's son, wrecked on the coast of France, was made prisoner by Guy of Ponthieu, ransomed from him by William of Normandy, and compelled—by a treachery which is the worst of many blots on William's splendid fame—to take a solemn oath that he would aid the Norman's designs on the English throne.

On his return to England, Harold found all Northumbria in revolt against the nameless cruelties of his savage brother Tostig, who, unable to face the universal hatred he had provoked, was fain to take refuge in Flanders; and then, as Kenneth and Fillan were about to sail on their usual voyage to Norway, they learned in the spring of 1066 that King Edward the Confessor had died that winter; that Harold, Godwin's son, had been crowned in his stead; and that the new king, wishing to strengthen himself by an alliance with the young earls of Mercia, had married their widowed sister Aldyth, our heroes' former hostess at Pen-maen-mawr.

All the years that had gone by since Hardrada's return from the East had left few traces on his comely face and giant form. Only by a few tell-tale threads of silver in his golden locks could one guess that he had passed his fiftieth year; and as he and his Scottish friends stood side by side on the brow of a sea-fronting cliff, before the long, low shed of tarred planking that served him as a palace, they looked up at his mighty figure as admiringly as ever.

" Every time I see your faces, lads," said the sea-king, laying a hand kindly on each man's shoulder, " my heart warms as it did when we slid off yon chain in the harbour of Mickle-gard, and were free at last of the Greeks and their rogueries. But what ship is yonder that buffets the waves so stoutly? By her build she should be French or Norman."

In fact, though a heavy sea was running, the

strange ship fought her way gallantly against it, and ere long was safely moored in the roadstead below.

"Go thou down, Anlaf," said the king, "and see what men they be. They shall be welcome, come they in peace or in war," added he with a grim smile.

Anlaf vanished down the rock-cut steps that led to the harbour, and soon returned with a tall and stalwart man, whose face was beautiful as a Greek statue, and framed in long curled hair. But even in its beauty there was something sinister and terrible, and to the keen Scots that low frowning forehead and those restless eyes told their own tale.

"Yon man is comely; but I like him not," whispered Kenneth to Fillan.

"Nor I," said Fillan in the same tone; "for methinks evil comes with him."

Kenneth started slightly, for he had had the same thought himself.

"Hail to thee, Harold of Norway!" cried the stranger. "Thou hast heard of me, belike. I am Tostig, Godwin's son, of Northumbria."

"Thou art welcome," said the Norse king, so frankly that only the practised ears of the Scots detected the slight want of cordiality in his tone. "Sit down and eat," he added, leading the way into his timber palace, "and then shalt thou tell thy business."

Tostig's business, when told, was so private that not even the trusty Scots were allowed to hear it. But there was good reason for this caution, for the traitor's errand was to invite Hardrada to invade and conquer England.

"I went to William the Norman," said he; "but though he be keen for it, he can do naught without his barons, and they will not be easily moved to such an emprise beyond the seas. Then hied I to Sweyn of Denmark, and bade him subdue England as did his uncle Knut [Canute]. And what was the craven's answer? 'A great man was Knut, a small man am I; yet even he had to fight hard for England when he had gotten it. Better keep safe that I have than by grasping at more risk losing all.' Wherefore I am come at the last to thee, the best warrior the northern lands have ever known; and I wot *thou* wilt not say nay."

Not a word said Hardrada while Tostig spoke, or even when he ended; and as he sat there in silence, with his massive head resting thoughtfully on his strong right hand, his own life and the future of

Norway itself—little as he guessed it—hung swaying
in the balance while he paused.

"Bait not thy hook for me with fair speeches,"
said he at last, abruptly and almost roughly; "such
food is not for bearded men. Till now, by land and
by sea, abroad and at home, all hath prospered with
me; and it is not well to tempt good luck too far.
Give me somewhat sure to rest on, or I stir not; for
well saith the old rede that we should be as young
men to execute, but as old men to resolve."

Brute and ruffian as he was, Tostig could be shrewd
enough when his own interest was concerned; and
the arguments that he put forward might have
persuaded a man far less willing to be convinced than
Harold Hardrada.

A treasury drained by King Edward's profitless
waste; an ill-guarded coast; an unfortified land; a
nation used to see Dane or Norseman give the law
to them as the fortune of war favoured him; and in
the district where they would land, half the popula-
tion inclining to the invaders as kinsmen, while the
other half dreaded their prowess as foes.

But the renegade's strongest argument was his last:

"Forget not that William the Norman hath his
eye on the same prize, and he is not a man to dally
when there is work in hand."

In a word, the traitor prevailed over the hero; and that autumn Harold Hardrada, with Fillan and Kenneth Macduff, sailed against England with a fleet of three hundred warships, the best that Norway could supply.

CHAPTER XXVI.

THE BRIDGE OF THE DERWENT.

HARDRADA and Tostig (who had joined him in the Orkney Isles) landed at Cleveland, and made short work of all opposition.

Some of the English fought valiantly, and died where they stood; but others were half-hearted in their resistance to the dreaded Norsemen, whom they held to be invincible. And not a few of the defenders had Norse or Danish blood in their veins, and, as Tostig had foretold, were more inclined to greet the invaders as kinsmen than to fight them as foes.

No small part of these joined Hardrada at once, and thus strengthened, the conquerors, flushed with success, advanced on Scarborough. But here the walls were strong, and the townsmen resolute; and in reply to a summons to open their gates, they sternly bade the besiegers "come and do it themselves."

But Harold Hardrada was not a man to be easily baffled. Mounting the steep hill that overhung the town, he and his men kindled a huge fire on the top, and with their spears tossed the burning wood on to the thatched roofs below. House after house took fire, as in the doomed Sicilian town long ago, till the whole city was one roaring blaze, through which the fierce Northmen burst in with a mighty shout, rushing to and fro in quest of booty amid surging flames and falling timbers as if they bore a charmed life.

Ere sunset all was over, and where a flourishing town had lately stood there was nothing left but blood and ashes.

Seldom, indeed, in that fierce age, did any man trouble himself about the justice of a quarrel where there was a good fight to be had; but even the habits of a lifetime could not save Macduff and Fillan from feeling disturbed at the sight of all this havoc and ruin.

" We are wasting the land that sheltered my father in his need and welcomed us when we had escaped the sea," said Kenneth. " Comrade, I like it not."

" It is too late for such thoughts now," said Fillan gloomily. " We have opened the flask, and we must drink the wine."

It was too late indeed, for their march on York was suddenly barred by Queen Aldyth's brothers, the young earls Edwin and Morcar, with all the "tall men of York" and many a stout Saxon from the country round.

It was a hard fight while it lasted, but it did not last long. Once more the headlong Norse valour bore down all before it; and foremost in the fray was Tostig, who, villain as he was, had all the courage of his race—the sole virtue, in truth, of this double-dyed traitor and murderer.

Beaten and broken, the poor remains of the Saxon host fled back to York, and the panic-stricken city agreed to surrender on the following day.

Next morning found Hardrada and half his army —the rest being with the ships a few miles off—encamped on the Derwent at Stamford Bridge, seven miles from York, which they were to enter in triumph that day. But to the surprise and disquiet of the two Scots, their old comrades, Biorn Hare-foot and Nine-man-Mord, so far from being blithe and exultant as might have been expected, were as silent and gloomy as themselves.

"I have had an ill dream," said Hare-foot moodily, when our heroes took notice of this. "I dreamed yesternight that a witch wife stood on a rock as our

ships went by, with a fork in one hand and a trough
in the other; and on the stern of each ship sat a
raven, and the witch cried to them, 'Be of good
cheer, my children, for all who sail in these ships
shall be your food.' "

"And I," cried Mord, "dreamed that before our
host went a witch wife riding on a wolf; and she
cast into his open jaws the carcass of a man, and
then another, and another, till all were swallowed up.
I saw her throw him thine, Saemund, and thine,
Sweyn, and thine, Biorn, and mine own likewise; and
as he ate she sang,—

> ' Grim wolf, fill thy maw,
> For enow shall there be,
> Hungry jaw, hairy paw,
> Both for thee and for me !' "

The superstitious hearers shuddered as they listened.
But they soon had something else to think of, for just
then a great cloud of dust began to roll up toward
them from the direction of York.

"What men come yonder ? " said Hardrada to Tostig,
as they stood side by side in front of their host.

" Friendly English coming to join me, no doubt,"
said Tostig carelessly.

But as the cloud came nearer, through it broke
" the shine of weapons like the glancing of ice ; " and

when the wind rent the dusty veil for a moment, all could see plainly the dragon standard of the Saxon!

"No friends these, but stout foes!" cried the Norse king. "Advance my banner, lads, and close your ranks around it."

Then having sent off three of his swiftest runners to bid the men who had been left with the ships come up at once, he took his post by the "Earth-Waster" banner, and his Norsemen formed around him in a vast circle, the points of their levelled spears bristling in one unbroken hedge of glittering steel.

Meanwhile the Saxon army, now full in view, halted and ranked itself in turn in front of the Norsemen's iron ring; and all at once a group of riders were seen to quit the English ranks and move toward the invaders.

Stepping forward to survey them, Hardrada stumbled and fell.

A shiver ran through the superstitious Norsemen at what they deemed a specially evil omen, and the foremost Saxon rider said quickly to the man at his side,—

"Knowest thou, Haco, who was yon tall man who fell but now?"

"That man," said Haco, "was King Harold Hardrada of Norway himself."

"He is a goodly man and a strong; but methinks his luck has forsaken him."

Then riding up to that part of the Norse line where Tostig's standard floated, the speaker called out in a clear, strong voice,—

"Stands Tostig, son of Godwin, by his banner? If so, let him hear me."

Prompt at the word forth came Tostig, bedecked and bedizened as was his wont.

"Greeting to thee from thy brother King Harold of England.   Thus saith he: 'Why should the sons of one mother be at strife?   Make peace, and thou shalt have Northumbria again, if the Northumbrians will receive thee; and if not, thine shall be all the lordships which the king had promised to his brother Gurth.'"

"It is well spoken," said Tostig, seeming to hesitate, as if he foresaw what tremendous consequences hung upon his decision.

But just then the Norse king's giant form came striding up to the spot to learn the meaning of this parley, and Tostig, seeing him, said quickly,—

"And if I accept, what will King Harold give to my friend and ally Harold Hardrada of Norway?"

The Saxon looked full at Hardrada's mighty bulk, and replied with stern calmness, loud enough for all around to hear,—

"Seven feet of English land for a grave, or as much more as his greater stature may demand."

"Go back then, and make ready for battle," cried Tostig fiercely. "Never shall it be said that I drew Harold, Sigurd's son, hither to aid my cause, and then cast him off and betrayed him."

The great sea-king looked hard after the Saxon envoy as he rode off, and turning to the still chafing Tostig, asked quickly,—

"Who was yon Englishman who spake so free and bold?"

"My brother, King Harold of England," replied the Saxon chief.

"Ha!" said the giant thoughtfully, "he was shorter than some of us; but firmly he rode, and firmly he spake."

A few minutes later a mighty shout told that the two armies had closed.

The Saxon horsemen came charging on the northern spears; but the ring held firm, and shaft and javelin from within smote down many a bold rider, amid shouts of taunting laughter from the triumphant Norsemen.

But there was a method in this seeming madness. The Saxon king (a great general as well as a stout soldier) had shrewdly calculated that the hot-blooded

Norsemen, fired with the fury of battle, and misled by the seeming ease with which they had beaten off the assaults of his cavalry, would, sooner or later, break their iron ring and rush to the attack.

The event proved that he was right. All at once, with a shout like the roar of a stormy sea, the Norse warriors broke loose, and came rushing on pell-mell in one huge, disorderly mass.

It was a fatal error. Instantly the English king and his foot soldiers, in firm array, fell like a thunderbolt on the disordered foes, rending them asunder as the wedge rives the oak ; and Harold had all but cut his way to the " Earth-Waster " standard when the fight suddenly took a new turn.

Forth from beneath his banner sprang Hardrada himself, flung away his shield, and wielding his mighty sword with both hands, " he smote and slew and all to-brake, as were he wode " (mad). Against those terrific strokes neither helmet nor shield availed, and the bravest Saxons went down before him like grass before the scythe, and through the breach he had made his wild men came bursting like a wave, bearing down all before them.

One moment more and the battle would have been lost ; but just then, as of old, " a certain man drew a bow at a venture," and his arrow found a mark for which it was never meant. Pierced through the throat, Hardrada flung his arms up convulsively, and fell to the earth a dead man. And at that sight burst from his men a cry so terrific in its utter agony and despair that for a moment it silenced even the roar of battle.

So died the last of the sea-kings.

It is needless to dwell on the ghastly details of that great day of slaughter, the Flodden Field of Norway. The Norse reserves, hurrying up in disorder, only swelled the red gleaning of that fell harvest of death; and the end of that dismal story is best told in the terrible simplicity of the old chronicler's own words :—

"And when the king fell, then Earl Tostig took the Earth-Waster banner, and held it up till he died. Then Eystein Orre took it, coming up hot from the ships, and he died likewise. Then they all died, for they would take no mercy. They threw off their mail, and fought bare-breasted till they were all dead together."

A single Norse champion, covering the retreat of his few surviving comrades, defended the Derwent bridge (like a second Horatius) against the whole pursuing host, and slew with his own hand nine-and-thirty Saxons. At last, disdaining all offers of mercy, he fell by a well-aimed javelin, and with him died the last hope of Norway.

"Kenneth Macduff, is it thus that I meet thee again?" said a familiar though long-unheard voice in our hero's ear, as he came to himself from the stunning shock of the blow that had struck him down as he bestrode the body of his friend Fillan.

Over him bent a calm and kindly face framed in snow-white hair, which, in spite of the jewelled mitre and rich robes, he knew at once for that of his old friend "Ailred the monk," who had fulfilled the elder Macduff's prophecy by becoming Archbishop of York.

Beside the archbishop stood a tall man in Saxon armour, whose face was so grand in its calm dignity that the shrewd Scot felt at once that this was no common man; nor was he, for he was no other than King Harold of England.

"What!" cried the king, "is this the son of Thane Macduff of Fife? The more do I marvel, then," he added, as he helped Macduff to rise, "that the son should come to waste a land that sheltered the father."

"Just is thy rebuke, King Harold," said the Scot, with a clouded brow; "but I did it for Harold of Norway, the truest friend that ever man had."

Harold Godwin's son's noble face clouded in its turn.

"Would that he could have been spared!" said he sadly; "but it might not be. Nathless, we will seek out his corpse, and give it such honours as are a brave man's due."

"And fear not for thy comrade, my son," added Ailred, as he caught Kenneth's anxious glance at the prostrate Fillan; "for, God be praised, he liveth. Bide thou here with him till we return."

But the seekers had not far to go, for only a few paces away, by his fallen standard, was the man they sought.

There he lay, the mighty conqueror, the terrible champion, the daring rover, struck down in the height of his pride and glory by an unknown hand, itself unconscious of the deed. "Seven feet of English land," and no more, had that strong arm and fiery spirit conquered; and that wonderful career that was the marvel of the whole world had ended in this.

The fatal shaft had spared that comely face, and there was a sad and solemn beauty in the stillness of the massive features that would never move again.

"They that take the sword shall perish by the sword," said Ailred sadly, as he looked down on the fallen giant. "May God forgive him, for he was a brave man."

"Amen!" said the king. "What ho! my men, bear his corpse back to his people, and tell them they are free to depart for their own land when they will, unmolested by me and mine."

As he said, so it was done, and the morrow's sunrise glanced on the receding sails of the invaders, bearing home the corpse of their bravest king from the land they had come to conquer. But the Saxon king's greatest triumph was his last. Nineteen days later he and his brothers, with the flower of English manhood, lay dead on the field of Hastings, and with them died Saxon England.

"Ailred the Good" survived his country's fall, and lived to denounce to his face, amid all his men of might, the terrible Conqueror himself. But William, with all his craft and cruelty, could appreciate true courage, and he heard the brave old man's rebuke in silence, and sent him away unharmed.

Fillan, luckier than his friends Mord, Sweyn, Biorn, and Saemund, who had all fallen around their king, recovered from his wounds to live many a happy year on "the bonnie braes o' Lochaber," whither he brought home as his bride the orphan daughter of King Gryffyth of Wales, whom he had saved in her infancy from the wolf of Pen-maen-mawr. From this union sprang in after days the

Stuart kings, who so long ruled first Scotland and then Scotland and England.

Earl Macduff of Fife died full of years and honours, and his son Kenneth succeeded him. But though no one stood more manfully for his country than he, Hardrada's career had taught him to prefer peace to war; and to his wise encouragement was due the rise of those settlements of industrious Flemings on the east coast of Fife, which were one day to be such a boon to that half-barbarous region. What the Fife men themselves thought of him may be gathered from the fact that, for many a year after his death their customary blessing on a newly-baptized son was this,—

"May God make thee such a man as our good Earl Kenneth!"

THE END.